*Return
to the Shadows*

Return
to the Shadows

ROBERT SERUMAGA

Atheneum NEW YORK 1970

1   The road was a narrow and dusty track in the
    countryside. There are many roads like it in
    Adnagu, strips of dust that wind through the tall
grass. Standing on top of one of the surrounding hills you
see only what comes within your focus, a pale brown belt
across the green fields. In the dry season the dust settles
on the blades of grass, soaking up the morning dew. Emerg-
ing from the mysteries behind the hill on one side, it crosses
your vision and disappears into the enigmas behind the
hills on the other side.

Thirty years ago on this road a messenger ran, his tattered shirt blowing in the wind, carrying in his hand the
news of the birth of a nameless infant. It was on the same
road five years later that this infant, now named Joseph
Musizi, sat in the back of his father's Dodge held in his
seat by a sobbing nurse, as the driver sullenly hurried in
the hope that the young child would just be in time to
attend the last few minutes of his father's life. They were
too late.

Another twenty-five years had passed, and Joseph
Musizi was on the same road again, harassed by fate, and
with him Simon Mutuba; two men thrown together by
events, or by some ill-meaning manipulator playing about
with the destinies of men. They were figures on the
road, walking, stumbling and still walking on. Behind

them lay danger and destruction; and in front of them hope.

They trudged on silently, listening to their own thoughts; occasionally they would need the reassurance of the other's voice, 'Joe?'

'Yes, Simon?' Again the silence would return; but it would not sound like a mere silence between words, or the gap between two breaths. It would be the silence of a breath stopped or the pause that precedes a jump when the man sees the rocks below the precipice. The breath stopped, becomes a sigh: 'Ah, forget it. It was a silly question. It leads nowhere.' For both Joe and Simon knew that these were questions to which answers lay in oneself, the discovery of the truth about one's existence.

What is truth? Another man, in another place and in another century had asked this question, but had not even waited to hear the answer. There were crowds to distract his attention, shout his decision for him and fetch him the water to wash his hands. But after a while on this lonely road on which they walked, the ear becomes used to the bird noises and the sound of the wind. Secluded, the mind turns on itself and questions things within. The result is a silence which belies internal commotion. They had been walking for hours now since they last stopped to ask for a drink of water. The skin was peeling off Simon's left small toe, just where it rubbed against the inside of the shoe. Joe himself was limping slightly. He had water on the right knee; or else what was that dull, pulsating pain? He tried to ease the weight as he walked, distorting his gait. The road did not help either. It had grown old with the years. The running water of the heavy rains had cut small valleys in its surface, and in between the winding ravines there were bumps which hurt your foot. Joe felt like a fly walking on his grandmother's wrinkled face.

Occasionally Joe would raise his forehead to the sun, whose scorching grin made the air around him tremble and his eyes gummy. Through the haze of dust and pain he would gaze at the twin hills beyond. Their green was dark and their surface rounded by the light mist of the distance. There was hope there for Simon and Joe, fugitives from the political upheaval in the city, on which they had now turned their backs. In the hills there were trees, with nests that sheltered real birds. But in the city the tree is a rock of steel and concrete and the nest harbours a machine-gun with death in its laughter and there is always a man to trigger its metal ribs with a murderous tickle.

Suddenly the silence was broken by a loud buzz above their heads. In one sweep Simon leaped, pushing Joe. Both men fell to the ground, their faces in the dust. Almost at the same time a small plane swooped down from a height and came low above their backs. As it tilted a man craned his neck and looked at the two prostrate figures. They did not see him; but in the distant the aircraft seemed to hover above them, they could feel their muscles tightening in readiness for the hot lead of the guns. Maybe the pilot had nothing to do with them, or he may have thought they were corpses, for he pulled up again and they heard the sound fade away and disappear in the distance. The glimpse that Simon had had of the machine made him certain it was a military aircraft. So the army had followed them, even to this lonely road?

3

'It was them,' Simon stammered at Joe. 'I wonder what they're looking for. Not us. We've done nothing!'

'We have,' Joe replied in despair. 'We ran away, and we must find ourselves before they find us.' It was true that they were now two men lying in the dust, but they had been different yesterday. Joe was a lawyer, economist and rich businessman, while Simon was his houseboy. Today they were companions, in search of survival.

This was a metamorphosis which had started long before the latest *coup d'état* three days ago when soldiers had raided Joe's house. In the midst of this confusion Joe had asked his servant to come with him and both men had tried to escape by car. At a roadblock they lost their car to the service of the army and the long walk had started towards the home of Joe's mother. Somewhere in a corner of Joe's mind remained a small cell of doubt and suspicion which multiplied its cancerous growth by the minute. Maybe the *coup d'état* was not the reason for this pilgrimage at all. Yes, more probably, the journey had started years ago when a creeping sense of disillusion had overtaken Joe, although he had been unaware of its beginning. This metamorphosis was to continue but no one could tell where it would end. Like the road on which they now walked, the story stretched behind them and in front of them, joining with other bigger roads and stories and leading to greater mysteries beyond.

'He's gone,' Simon said.

'What?'

'I said I don't think he'll come back.'

'Oh, he'll come back all right. If not today, tomorrow. If not tomorrow, next year.'

'And if we get up and walk now,' said Simon, 'we'll get to your mother's house before next year.'

Joe smiled, but the smile did not reach his lips. 'I suppose you're right,' he said as both men got off the ground, back on to their sore feet. The sweat again began to flow down on Joe's face instead of on to the ground as it had done when he was prostrate. He pulled his shoulders forward slightly, making his shirt touch his back to mop the sweat. Though this dried his back, he could not do it too often, as his stiff collar had by now made inroads in to his neck causing a burning pain. This he made worse every time he moved his shoulders. They began to walk again. As they did, Joe felt his physical pain intensified by this growing nagging feeling in his head: 'You're running away, Joe; you're running away from your proper responsibilities.'

What good would it do to stay and fight? Get snuffed out without trace in the winds of turmoil – unlamented, unremembered. You must run away and stay to fight another day. But when? When all the goodness is gone and evil inhabits the land. Yet to fight without weapons is merely false heroism. Or is it? A stone is a weapon even against a machine-gun. Is it really now? But he had tried before and the spade had turned into a snake as he shifted the rubbish. Was he at last powerless? Were even his intellectual rationalizations and cynical explanations unable to bring him relief?

'Hell, Simon, why don't you say something? This journey is long, and silence makes it longer.'

But Simon was also wrapped in his own thoughts. In the silence Joe felt his hand go to his thigh. A thought or

5

memory was coming to him. So his hand went to his thigh to make a note of it. It was his habit. He always made his mental notes on his leg, scribbling with his index finger, illegibly yet indelibly. Before he knew it he was writing: 'Sadness is the feeling of impotence,' and in brackets, (Spinoza). Then 'Pleasure is the consciousness of vital effort (Kant).' He continued: 'Ideas are acts conscious of their direction, quality and intensity.' He could not remember who said that but wrote further: 'Feeling is confused knowledge. Pleasure and pain arise from confused representation which makes known to us the increase or decrease in our vitality.' There it was – pain. He could even define the damn thing if he wanted to. For a moment he had the illusion that he had thereby gained control of it. But his knee and his neck easily dispelled the illusion. He wondered what Simon would say if he told him: 'My sensibility is registering a decrease in my vitality due to the combined effects of my stiff collar rubbing for too long against my neck, and the water on my knee.' Simon would not even understand that, and he seemed none the worse for it. So he said to him instead: 'How is your small toe?'

'Still painful, boss.'

Joe did not like the 'boss' especially under the new circumstances. He noted further: 'Eight wasted years spent in a classroom in Europe.' Even as he wrote Simon had that distant look again. What the hell was Simon thinking? He was there with him and yet miles away. Was he despising Joe, his master, for running away? But how could he sit in judgement? He obviously did not know all the facts: he had only heard rumours, scraps of information that distort the awareness of the mind. For a moment Joe

6

felt the question come to his lips. But he resisted it. He was not going to ask Simon for judgement. He had made the decision himself and that was that. Nobody had the right to question his good faith. For, to understand, one would probably have to have lived Joe's life. Such is life that, having lived the experience, the mind is confused by the pain, and objective logic is abandoned for a more pervasive, less rationalized reaction. It was only fair to leave the matter in the hands of the person who bears the pain.

The decision: let fate run its course, get a small area of safety for yourself and hold on to it. The world beyond, its sufferings and its glories, are only the macabre orchestrations of a band of inherently imperfect men. One's duty was to seek a little comfort and not be sacrificed on the altar of an idealism pursued by creatures so obviously unworthy of such providence.

That was no easy way out either. Joe had come to that conclusion after long periods of agonized thought and painful introspection. His earlier life apart, there was the immediate problem of survival. Ever since Joe had returned from studies in Europe, full of revolutionary spirit he had suffered a number of disappointments which had turned him into himself. He had seen several *coups d'état* in his country, each one more futile and destructive than the last. It was during these that he developed what he called his *coup d'état* drill. At the drop of a coup, he would get out of town fast and run to the safety of his country home. Later, when the dust had settled, he would return to town for the trials of the former ministers. That is if they were caught at all. For they had learnt the tricks themselves: one pound for the home bank and one for the Swiss bank, and a gentleman thief, turned politician's friend, could organize escape routes for a modest fee. Often a few ministers would be caught and brought to trial, alive if possible. Joe had often been counsel for the defence in these dramas before the men were shot. He earned a good amount that way, but at times he twitched nervously when he compared himself to the man who organized escape routes.

This time, however, Joe had not been so lucky and they had passed through thirty-six hours of hell. He was shaken to the roots and was on the verge of being forced to think again; observe in a new light, redefine, reassess and then find a new path to victory, to defeat or to obliteration; where would the honour be? The world is flat and round, and there are lots of ideals in heaven; on earth there is the pain of imperfection and the illusion of perfection. Perhaps the conflicts would soon resolve and the truth will stand revealed.

Nothing was clear yet; everything was in a state of dissolution. Joe and Simon knew little about the nature of the upheaval from which they were running. All they knew was what news Simon had picked up at the butcher's shop the morning after the night of the coup. It was little and it did not explain the strange events of the previous night.

Simon had been awoken by the sound of somebody pulling the chain in his lavatory. He had walked out into the garden at the back of his master's house, where he had met a madman and a soldier. As he walked along this road with Joe he still puzzled about what these men had said and done to him. When he had woken up in the morning, his master Joe was lying on a wet floor, with broken glass all around him.

And as for Joe, he knew that soldiers had come to his house and drunk his brandy. Then suddenly they had knocked him out. He had been unconscious for nearly ten hours, but he was sure he had seen the strangest things during that time. He kept referring to what the 'shadows had told him'; this only confused Simon further as he knew nothing of what Joe had seen while unconscious. So he thought it must have been the condition his master had been in when he found him on the floor which was the cause of his madness. But was it really madness?

Simon retraced the story over and over in his mind. He still was puzzled. He had found Joe lying on the floor; he had tried to get up, but had reeled over and fallen. Then he had said: 'Where are the shadows? I want them to tell me some more.' His eyes had looked like holes without pupils. He was seeing something but it must have been far away in the distance. But before Simon could get him to say any more, he had snapped out of his condition. Then he had said: 'You won't understand, Simon. Come on. Help me up.' He had asked Simon to make a bed for him, and had slept without stirring for a long time. When he had woken up they had started out on this journey. Simon wished Joe would tell him more.

'I think it's going to rain,' Joe finally said to Simon.

'What's that?' Simon asked, recovering himself.

'The clouds, the dark clouds.'

As Joe said that, the rainy cloud which had been gathering moved across the face of the sun. The shadow which embraced them was followed by a cool breeze. The effect was strangely uplifting but it was an illusion, for it was just a breeze and a shield from the direct rays of the sun. Everything else remained the same. Instinctively they began to look for a shelter from the coming rain.

'There's no house around here, Simon.'

'No, there isn't,' Simon replied.

As if by design, their eyes turned together to the shelter of a large tree in the field to their left just as the skies rumbled a distant warning, a crack of thunder followed and the waters came down. Simon and Joe dashed and took shelter under the tree. But the wind blew drops of rain making them wet even as they sat there.

As the water dripped on to Joe's face, washing the accumulation of dust down his cheeks, Simon began to see him as he had never seen him before. It had always been Joe the boss; returning from work, with Simon hurrying up to the car to open the door and take the groceries to the kitchen; sitting in the velvet emerald green sofa and calling out to Simon to bring out some brandy. There was no resentment but by seeing themselves solely as master and servant they had failed to notice themselves as two human beings. If you had asked Simon how tall Joe was, he would never have been able to tell you.

Now as they were sitting under a tree to keep off the rain, with all their possessions and trappings behind them, Simon saw his master. He also suspected that Joe was looking at him afresh. Joe was six foot tall with a gold-brown complexion. In normal life his eyes would be big and clear and his hair dark, with a parting on the left-hand side. Now his tall frame had developed a stoop, his hair was dishevelled, the colour of his skin was disguised under a layer of dust and rain and his eyes were almost closed to keep out the wind and the water.

Simon was about five foot six with a brown to black complexion, small eyes and slightly exaggerated ears. He never bore himself upright. Maybe it was the effect of his being a servant, a calling he never suspected would be his. What difference did it make now that they had seen each other physically. Was it just another instalment of useless information? Still it was good to know what a man really looked like.

Joe must have been very tired, or it might have been the effect of sitting down after being so long on his feet. For as Simon looked at him and the raindrops still beat down on his face, his eyes narrowed and his head drooped in slow nodding movements. This forced back the questions Simon was about to put to him about the night of the *coup*. Instead he ran through his memory for extra bits of information.

He was sure one of the men he had seen in the back garden that night had had a gun, but he had not fired it. Then that prophet or madman, dressed in banana leaves? Maybe it was a dream, an omen as to what was going to happen in the morning. The first Simon had heard of the *coup* was in the morning following this strange night. The announcement had come through the window from a neighbour's radio. Simon had been cleaning the house after making the bed for his dazed master. 'Attention everybody! All people going to work must take care not to carry offensive weapons of whatever kind on their persons. Anybody found in possession of these weapons will be arrested and questioned. The new Government wishes you a very good morning.' Then the martial music had resumed. It was then that Simon had begun to think he might know who might have attacked Joe and knocked him on to the floor where he had found him.

After he had cleaned the house, Simon decided to ride on his bicycle to the city to find out exactly what had happened. At the approach to the city he had found them. They were dressed in khaki. On their heads were steel helmets and grass. On their shoulders were bullets and in their hands guns with naked bayonets.

He knew them well and he also knew the feeling they gave him. They stared as he passed, grim and silent as the grave, which in a way they symbolized. He got off his bicycle though they had not ordered him to; something from within him forced him off; the desire to survive perhaps transmuted itself into a gesture of submission.

All he wanted to know now was who had taken over. You could never know that from the colour of a man's uniform. He had to go to the butcher's shop to find out. The butcher, a genial man in his early thirties, had political ideas, an affable personality and a natural knack for telling stories. News gathered around him and, after he had doctored it for comic effect, the truth could still be discerned beneath the surface.

There was an unusual atmosphere among the people gathered at the shop. They stood around in small clusters arguing in agitated but subdued voices. On the fringes a few of them gazed in silence into the distance. Simon approached them, inquiring and listening.

'They got him. The butcher. Those bastards got him,

and his wife and children too. Their bodies were found this morning.'

'But who killed him?' Simon asked.

'Where were you born, friend? Or has your mind stopped working?'

'Tell him it's the army; he wants to hear it.'

'Oh, shut up,' said a short grey-haired man.

'What I mean to say,' Simon was explaining, 'is which side has taken over which side?'

'This chap comes from the marshes, God help us! Haven't you heard? It's Brigadier Okum . . .'

'Field-Marshal Okum,' interrupted another with an informed air.

'What? Field-M — when did it happen?'

'He rechristened himself a little while ago.'

'Well, you heard it, all of you. It's the Marshal from now on. He has arrested all the politicians on the outside and he is releasing all those on the inside. Normal coup practice,' intoned the man with the informed air.

'Who gave you this news?' Simon asked.

'The butcher.'

'Before he died?'

'Of course not; after. Man, you speak like a foreigner. You see me with a calabash on my head and you ask whether there is beer where I am coming from.'

'I *am* a foreigner!'

'Oh, really? I beg your pardon.'

He was about to ask more questions when two army trucks arrived and vomited soldiers. The crowd looked as if they had seen death incarnate. Defenders of the peace had, here at the butcher's shop and in many parts of the land, come to represent death. They scattered all over the place: lying on the ground and taking aim, hiding behind walls and taking aim, behaving in a manner seldom associated with sane men. Then the voice came over a loud speaker: 'You are all hereby ordered to disperse. Under the Emergency Regulations just declared, all meetings of more than two people are strictly forbidden.'

The crowd began to disperse muttering with discontent.

'We can just about speak to our wives without committing an offence,' one man was heard to say.

'You have something to say, Mister?' a man with a gun inquired in a menacing voice, his lips trembling slightly beneath his moustache.

'No . . . er . . . what I was saying,' he fumbled under the weight of the soldier's hard look.

Two other soldiers closed in on him and lifted him into the truck. Nobody said it. But everybody knew that that was probably the last they would ever see of him. Along with the others and covered by about fifty guns, Simon got on his bicycle and went home.

Joe was just waking up at the house when Simon arrived back. He instructed Simon to pack a few things and get ready for the journey to the country home. They left soon afterwards with Simon this time sitting in the front with his boss.

As they went Simon told Joe what he had seen and heard. One of the things that Simon couldn't figure out even now was that Joe looked definitely more shocked than he would normally have been when Simon broke the news of the death of the butcher. Was it possible that at last death in others was beginning to break through the hard armour of

Joe's cynicism? The other thing was that Joe's face had seemed to light up when Simon had told him about his vision of a prophet in banana leaves. Simon had not connected it with anything really specific. Could it after all have been some kind of somnambulent madness. Yet Joe had looked as if something had clicked: something that did not appear to bear any firm relationship to the trend of events, but a scrap of information that tickles the subconscious without immediately enlightening the conscious mind. Some kind of snatch from a forgotten dream.

It was late in the evening and darkness was beginning to fall. So they would have to stop at the Savana Inn for the night for fear of the curfew. The loose stones on the road spread out and rumbled as Joe pulled up and stopped at the main gate. His lights struck a dark figure which waved a gun.

'Where you going?' the soldier asked.

'To the hotel. We wish to spend the night here and continue our journey in the morning.' But the voice said: 'You cannot do that.'

'I say . . . but we are regular clients here.'

'I said you cannot do that. The hotel has been taken over by the captain as Regional Command Headquarters. So you have to find somewhere else to stay.'

'But the curfew! You chaps will be the first to fire bullets at us if we go out in the dark.'

'Yes,' the soldier replied; a simple admission. No more.

'Then what do we do?'

'That's your problem. I've conveyed my order to you.'

There was a brief silence, then Joe said: 'Who do these

fellows think they are?' He made as if to get out of the car, but Simon restrained him. Instinct told him.

'But we are supposed to have certain rights in this place,' Joe said, and the silence made him look about himself, self-consciously.

They paused for a moment, not knowing exactly what to do. If they persisted they would probably be shot, and if they went out into the dark after curfew hours, they would be shot.

'This is ridiculous,' Joe was thinking to himself. 'We are supposed to know what we can do and what we cannot do. And if these men are going to stand there and order us around . . .'

'That's it, five minutes,' the soldier said looking at his watch.

'What about five minutes?'

'That's what I gave you. Now you can come out of that car.'

'But you never mentioned any five minutes.'

'I don't have to mention anything . . .'

'I say . . .'

'And you are not saying anything either. Now come out before I smoke you out.' The soldier meant business.

Simon, aware of the reputation of the soldiers, was fiddling with the door and trying to get it open. Joe sat tightly on his honour and his principle. He was not going to be pushed around. Certainly not in front of his servant. He took a cigarette from his pocket but, before he could light it, he was lying flat on the road, with the soldier standing above him, his bayonet ready to pierce.

'Don't do it, corporal,' a saving voice came from the

darkness around them. A torch waved its light. The voice belonged to the sergeant.

'Yes, sir,' the corporal came to attention, and ordered up his rifle. For Joe it was like re-living a dream, an experience which tends to intensify the lived moment. There was a deathly pause, and then:

'Corporal, take his car, we shall need it for operations. Where is the other one? Here, lock them both up in the wine cellar in the hotel: You'll let them go first thing in the morning.'

'Yes, sir.'

Joe just lay there on the road unbelieving. He did not dare to protest. Simon looked on with the expression of a man who had seen it all before in close intimacy. He could not help feeling sorry for his boss. He did not know how to let expediency supersede a principle in moments of personal bodily crisis.

The sergeant began to walk away. Then he turned back suddenly: 'Corporal, I've got a better idea. Don't lock them up. Just escort them to the outskirts of this town and let them go their way.' Simon was relieved to hear that. Joe was still too unbelieving to care what happened.

'Yes, sir.' The soldier moved briskly. He got into Joe's car, put both men in the back seat and drove them off to the edge of the town. There he left them, silent and incredulous. Simon and Joe both looked at the car as it drove away. A cloud of dust arose in its wake, lit by the red rear lights as the car disappeared into the distance. They stood petrified, two men getting away from trouble. Two men caught up by the hatred, jealousy and stupidity of the people with whom they shared a country. A man cannot run away from darkness. He can only light a candle against it, build an area of light in the midst of the forest; often the light is snuffed out, by the winds of discord, but its demise would be honourable. Yet men have acted differently; they have created the darkness and then retracted into the even darker interior of their shells. The darkness wants only to be feared not respected, and it feeds on the bones of those who in fear avert its embrace.

'I think we should start on our way, sir,' Simon said, but Joe was silent as he looked in the direction in which his car had disappeared.

'I said I think we should be on our way, sir.'

'Uh? Did you speak? I mean where to, where are we going?'

'We're going to the country home, sir.'

'Oh yes, that's right. You think it'll be safe there?'

'I don't know, sir.'

'Well somehow I don't think so. We seem to be followed by ill-luck in uniform. I think we had better try and make it to my mother's home. It's remote enough there. Anyway no soldiers will ever go to her house. She has nothing to do with politics.'

'All right, sir, but we'll have to go by the small paths in the villages. I wouldn't like to risk our necks on the open road. There're too many soldiers there.'

Joe slipped as they began to walk and held on to Simon for support. 'Do you think, Simon, this will ever stop?'

'I don't know, sir. Human greed knows no limits. As long as there are rich pickings to be had, men'll fight and kill each other. They've always done so.'

This was where the small paths had led them, after a

long night. Into the rain, under the branches of a tree, to shelter like birds of the forest. Simon, gazing at Joe, wondered if his mind was dreaming or just blank; he was being driven into an empty nap by sheer exhaustion. The rain was now clearing, and a drop of water hung precariously from the tip of Joe's nose as he nodded. One more drop of rain would have pushed it off. Simon looked at it for a moment and it began to irritate him. He was just about to yield to a temptation to make it drop when a drum sounded in the distance and Joe stirred. He sneezed instantaneously, scattering the drop, then looked at Simon with an apologetic grin.

'We'd better be on our way again,' Simon suggested; the drum sounded again almost at the same time. It came from the Mission. Maybe it was mid-day. They could not tell the time. Simon rose and, in the instant that Joe stayed sitting, he noted on his thigh as was his habit: 'For mine eyes *are* upon their ways: they are not hid from my face, neither in their iniquity hid from mine eyes (Jeremiah 16: 17).' For the men in Joe's country had wrought the pot upon the wheel, but they had let it drop from their hands and spoil. Other men picking it up to take it back to the wheel had done the same. That was why Joe was out in the rain.

Simon and Joe stepped out of the grass once more and on to the road. It was wet this time. The mud stuck on their boots, making their legs heavy; the harder they pulled to free their feet for another step, the more slippery the ground felt, and so they had to walk in short repetitive steps. But there was only one way to go, forward, to hope and safety; they had to get home where the long tether originates and pulls at their navels. There is peace; there is water to wash the dust and mud off the tired faces and a mother cooking plantains in a pot of groundnuts; goats eating the young banana shoots are chased away by children with laughter squeezing tears out of the sponges of their eyes.

They came round a bend and found themselves gazing at a trench dug in the middle of the road. A saboteur had been and gone; and was possibly in the neighbourhood, holding his breath. It seemed to Joe a long way to come to trap soldiers. One should dig these things in the middle of the streets in the city, not out in the deserted . . .

'Ssh, what's that?'

'The clouds again,' Joe said. 'Rain.'

'No it isn't.' It was drawing near, the menacing sound of a truck. 'Come on, Joe, we've got to get out of here.' Joe had no time to protest for Simon had grabbed and pulled him into the thick undergrowth to the right side of the road.

'What are you doing . . .?'

'Quiet, we're dead if they find us.'

Round the corner a truck full of soldiers appeared; it braked, and screeched to a stop right at the mouth of the gaping hole. Helmeted heads knocked against one another and cursed. Simon swallowed as he saw the truck safe by the trench. It was a disappointed gulp, like that of a man to whose mouth meat had been presented, and then withdrawn just as he was ready to savour it.

As the two men watched, a young officer jumped out of the vehicle and started giving fast crisp orders in English. Then he changed to another language which he spoke with difficulty. He had a babyish face with slightly over-emphasized lips and could not have been in the army for long; he was probably one of those who had been dropped into position from the heights of Sandhurst. His subordinates were much older, and many of them must have seen battle under a few flags, including that of the U.N. They would have entered the forces from somewhere in mid-primary school. Thereafter they would have snailed their way upwards until they hit the Sandhurst barrier. There they had probably stopped and turned bitter. The Sandhurst man was useful in as far as he could read maps where others found difficulty, but he remained an object of jealousy and intrigue. He knew it too. And it was this that made him wary underneath the tough officious exterior.

Was he out on a limb? Or had he succumbed to the temptations of office and the luxuries of independence. Or was he in fact not thinking about these things at all, just fighting as he was trained to, and leaving the moral decisions to others. Joe wondered from where he was crouched in the grass. For days now the soldiers had been in a fighting posture. One found it difficult to say they had been fighting, because though they had killed and mutilated, some of their victims could not have provided the other side to the fight. The young lieutenant had looked with a certain unease as his soldiers carried out their outrages but he had not intervened. Was he afraid? Or didn't he care at all? Perhaps he cared, and could in fact see some cruel justification in it all. I mean what does society expect of its soldiers? You take a group of young normal men and you give them a gun and a uniform. At the crack of dawn a bugle, the signal, and then all day you train them in the techniques of murder. But you go even further: you provide a whole philosophy, a complete rationalization to the simple acts of killing. You impart a dignity, a form of gallantry to the destruction of men who happen to be on the other side. To shoot, to kill, to maim and to survive. Then you find that when the killing has been done and the destruction complete, a soldier stands, dazed, before the society which forced his hand and warped his consciousness. He has seen the blood and the shit in the bowels of men. Faces that stared, their blankness a question in itself. Charred ruins of human bodies; and the children. Above all the children. What chance do they have?

Yet all around this young man, this soldier, are the cries of victory. He has won. For that, a medal. And for the murders, the blood, the staring eyes and the bodiless hand of a child holding a toy, well, he must bear that on his own shoulders. After all we all have a certain social responsibility. Carrying our share of the can. Anyway he needn't have done it all. Need he? Hell, I mean we all like victories, but . . . and when it has all been done and disowned, there stands the young man who in his misguided gallantry was pushed on to do our dirty work for us. There stands the soldier who must kill, but must not rape or even loot. Just kill. It's better. It's enough. From the hands of this young man, the blood trickles. Cold blood. Clotting, rotting. We cheer him and pin a medal on his chest, and bits of coloured ribbon. Our soldier.

And there, at the trench, the young commander watched his men carry out his orders. Were they aware of any moral obligations? No, it seemed. Just fighting machines. Somebody's son turned into a bloody fighting machine. He had watched their outrages and had felt the gap between him and them widening further every minute. It was the consciousness of this gap that had made him frightened of them. They wore the same battle-dress, but somehow they never really accepted him. If he were to moralize with them they might even get rid of him without batting an eyelid. The strange thing was that now that the gap seemed even wider, he felt less scared of them. It might have been that the desire to remain alive had been reduced in him by the disgust he felt for himself, or that the mounting hatred and contempt for the other soldiers told him they could do him no harm even if they tried. They could shoot and kill him, that's for sure; but he would really be dying a better death than the death he felt inside him now.

A bicycle-bell rang in the distance. The officer turned his head. It was like seeing an advertisement for the strength of the bicycle. A large man was carrying an even larger woman on the pillion; and a small girl with a face contorted by the painful pressure sat on the cross-bar. They approached and a soldier waved them to a stop. The man planted his legs on either side of the bicycle, but the weight must have been too great for his balance and they all fell over with a thump. The soldiers broke out into wild laughter. One of them approached the couple as they got up and shook off the dust.

'You can't ride a bicycle, can you?'

'No, sir, I fell.'

'I saw that. I have eyes. Now get over there and stand still.'

The man did as he was told. The soldier approached

the woman who, it now appeared, was around seven months pregnant. The other soldiers began to giggle and make indecent remarks. He looked at them and smiled mischievously. The husband's face began to twitch with fear of what might happen. The lieutenant looked as something inside him was saying: Not again, not this time, they cannot do it. But he was making no move. Fear gripped him again. The soldier touched the woman's chin.

'Get your hands off her you . . .'

'Shut up if you still want to live,' the soldier cut the husband short, gun menacingly pointing. The little girl began to sob. Another soldier approached her grinning at his friends as he did so. They giggled. Still the lieutenant just looked on. He hated himself, and thought he was going to bring up.

Suddenly a voice came through on the radio which one of the soldiers had been closely attending to all this time. They all stopped and looked at the radio. They had quizzical looks on their faces as if they could expect either victory or defeat, either to celebrate or to throw away their arms and run, according to the nature of the news. The radio operator listened carefully and then turning to the lieutenant handed him the receiver: 'Command headquarters, sir.' Grabbing the instrument the officer listened. The other soldiers looked on quietly. The voice was loud and clear. 'Have you found them?'

'Not yet, sir.'

'What've you been doing then, lieutenant? Drinking with the women in the villages?'

'No, er, I mean no, sir. We've looked everywhere, sir, where they could possibly go but . . .'

'That's it, isn't it. Now look where you think they couldn't go. You'll find them. They mustn't get away or we'll have a permanent revolution on our hands. Bring them back here, dead or alive.'

'Yes, sir.'

'Er, and lieutenant if you meet any resistance in the villages, don't pull your punches. Crush it! Crush it, so that nobody'll ever let the word resistance cross his mind.'

'Er, yes, sir.'

'What was that?'

'I said yes, sir.'

'Right, and report to me in half an hour.'

'Yes, sir.' The lieutenant handed the receiver back to the signal officer. He turned and faced the other soldiers. 'Now listen carefully, everybody. We've looked everywhere for the government men who escaped during the fighting. We've looked everywhere where we thought they might have thought we would think they would be going. And perhaps that is why we have not found them. Now we must look where they think we cannot think they could think of going. Is that clear?'

'Yes, sir.'

'Really? Well now, we leave the trucks here, since the road is not filled in. And we're going to search the undergrowth along the roadside from here to as far as the light of the sun will allow us to go. Now get cracking.'

They all sprang into formation and began to move towards the undergrowth. Joe and Simon wondered if this was the end. The lieutenant gave one look at the man and woman and their bicycle; he waited to let all the men go ahead. Suddenly he opened fire and mowed down the whole of his platoon. They went without a chance of firing back.

For a few minutes he stood there in disbelief at himself. The civilians with the bicycle stood and stared, not knowing whether to congratulate him or call for help. Over in the grass by the roadside, Joe had fainted convinced he had been shot and Simon was trying to revive him, silently.

Then the officer went over and looked at the bodies to see if anyone was still moving. None were. He slung the gun on his shoulder, looked at the distant mist and walked off towards it. He did not know yet where he was going. He just walked. And as he went, he sensed the heaviness of the heartlift and his pace quickened. There was freedom where only minutes previous he had felt like a trapped animal. They would probably get him eventually and hang him from the nearest tree. But then they would be killing a free man. It was much better that way.

Suddenly Joe came to life. He gave a shout, which fortunately the officer in the distance did not hear, jumped up and ran like mad farther into the bush. Simon followed, trying to grab him and restrain him, but without success. The man and woman thought these were two corpses come to life. They shouted and ran off, ululating and trying to shake their bodies free of some unknown flea of fear that had grabbed them.

2 After they had been running for some distance, Joe and Simon came upon some houses and they stopped. They were still wondering where on earth they were when a nun emerged from the back of one of the houses, threw out a basin of water and retreated.

They had arrived at the Mission. Joe's mother's house was not far now, but they had a little distance to go yet. Joe sat down panting and the pain returned to his knee. Why the hell had he run? He should have got hold of that officer and shaken his hand; then, maybe, he and the officer might have felt together.

'I wonder if we could find that young man again,' he said wincing from the pain in his knee.

'We ran away from him,' Simon replied.

'Hell, I know, Simon, but I mean . . .'

'Why did we run, Joe?'

'How should I know?'

'You were driven mad with fear, weren't you?' Perhaps Simon was looking for the final step-down by his master.

'Of course I wasn't. I just thought it prudent at the time.'

'Why? We didn't dig the trench . . .'

'Who pushed me into the grass in the first place?'

'I did, because I was frightened of the soldiers. Years ago in town they killed my father; he was alone in the house.'

'I'm sorry, Simon. You never told me this before.'

'So am I, Joe. Sorry, I mean, that we don't stay and

fight. That we always run away. Surely we've got every reason to fight.'

'Reason is a very tricky friend, Simon. It deserts one in moments of crisis. I thought I knew the answers, but that was before the night of the *coup* when the shadows spoke to me.'

'The shadows, Joe?'

'Yes, Simon, the shadows. But you'll not understand. It is hidden underneath the surface beyond those hills. Have you seen a hole in the horizon? No. And you haven't been pushed through the paths. Then how can I explain?'

'Joe, I think we should take a rest.'

'You don't believe in shadows, Simon, eh? Then why have you been stepping out of the paths of the whirlwinds all the time we have been on the road?'

'I never said I didn't believe. I only asked if we should take a rest.'

'I knew it, Simon. Superstition always looks strange in everybody but ourselves. There is a blind spot beneath the surface where the sun never shines. That's where the trouble starts.'

The clock must have struck four and brought the afternoon classes at the Mission School to an end, for just then the door burst open and out spilled shouting, chanting children. Joe and Simon moved from behind the banana trees at the backs of the houses where they had stopped and caught sight of the children going home from school. So they were even going to school. What does a change of politicians mean to them? It has happened so often before. An assassination, a few murders in the city, but school goes on. This had been Joe's school. Right now he wished he had stayed there for ever. But just then a big boy started running after a small one and pushed him into the grass. The small boy cried out.

'They start very young,' he said to Simon. 'I mean the thugs. We ought to get them early and nip them in the bud.'

'Yes,' Simon said without verve or enthusiasm, just plain agreement.

'Do you know Stephen Kiyonjo and Matthew Lwazi?'

'Yes, boss, er . . . I mean, Joe . . . er . . .' Simon was stopped by Joe's stare. After what they had been through, they had become Joe and Simon to each other. But Joe's mention of his two friends, their names and the tone of his voice had thrown Simon back in time: he servant, Joe boss.

'Hell, man, cut the boss bit will you?'

'I'm sorry,' Simon said without real remorse.

'Anyway as I was saying, Stephen and Matthew and I were here at school together, years ago. I wonder what happened to Katende?'

'Who?'

'I don't think you know him. The bully with the big knuckles.'

Simon did not reply. There was silence and then Joe nearly mentioned the butcher: his other school mate, but he thought better of it. I mean how much can you tell Simon, even at a moment like this. He stared at his old school as the freshness and pain of nostalgia embraced him. Up on the veranda of the Father's house, a priest in white robes was walking to and fro; must be reading his breviary. I wonder why he has to do it walking to and fro like that.

Could be part of the prayer or something. Now if it had been at another time and another goddam day they might have been prepared for it, and he and Simon would have scared the hell out of that nun with her basin of water. Just like old times, with big Katende. Do you know, nuns have their baths with their clothes on! Anyway that's what old Katende used to say. Now come to think of it, if that soldier at the house hadn't had a scar, he might have looked exactly like Katende. That must have been it. That feeling of partial recognition. He and that Madalena woman. . . . Jesus, that Madalena must have died years ago. She nearly had him killed; and all because of a weed. It was a green weed, a climber with yellow flowers and shining dark green leaves. This weed had led to a beating by his teacher Mr Lizard. Even now Joe thought it was really the fault of that old woman Madalena. Most mornings Joe had met Madalena as he went to serve mass in the early hours. People said she attended mass every single day of the year; if she did she must have been a very tough woman for when Joe first saw her she was getting close to seventy. Only her wrinkled face and her slightly unsteady gait betrayed her age. As she walked she took a fold of her long dress, squeezed it in the palm of her left hand and held the hand behind her back. In her right hand she always carried rosary beads and her mouth moved in perpetual prayer. This was the cause of great difficulty to Joe on several occasions. He always met her going in the opposite direction because she attended the first mass and he went to the second one which was not so early in the morning. So whenever he met her he stopped for a moment as if to salute her but, seeing her lips in prayer, he would start off again as fast as he had stopped. Madalena did not like this. She thought it her right to be saluted by the young people of the village. So she told his grandmother what an ill-mannered brat her grandson was. His grandmother told Joe that she did not know what was becoming of him, passing by old Madalena without so much as a 'Good morning'. Did he want people to say, when Madalena died, which must be soon, that his own grandmother had killed the old woman?

So the next time Joe met her, he stopped and said good morning, whereupon Madalena gave him a lecture: 'Do I look to you like a woman who has grown mad from old age? Or do you think my head has been sprouting mushrooms from too much water on the brain? Let me tell you, son of a puff-adder, that head of yours is full of nothing but mildew. Disturbing me in the middle of my prayers. Didn't you see my lips moving?'

'But you yourself said to my grandmother . . .'

'Don't you grandmother me! That woman has a mouth full of flies because she cannot keep it shut. And don't you answer me back. This thing I saw born yesterday; yes I did; and I saw your mother urinate on your head as she brought you from her womb; now you come and disturb me in the midst of my Hail Marys. You ought to be ashamed of yourself.'

She broke off suddenly and went away, leaving young Joe utterly astounded. He stopped briefly to recover and then continued on his way to the church.

This experience would not have caused him to resent the old woman as much as he did later, had she not gone and reported him to his teacher over the weed. The stink of this green weed with its yellow flower had got for it the name of sezimana, or 'the vaginal weed'. Joe's grand-mother had forbidden him to use the obscene name! 'Don't ever let me hear that word cross your lips or I'll rub the teete grass over them till they bleed. It's called "The weed that drives away leopards".' But that was such a long name and she did not explain why and how this weed chased away leopards. Later, a boy at school told him that every time the leopard smelled the weed, it thought there were people around somewhere making love so it ran away. This did not satisfy Joe either. One day it rained in the after-noon and it was mostly after the rain that this weed gave off the strongest scent. So after school, Joe was going home with the other children in a light drizzle, and they were all singing:

> *The rain is falling*
> *The sun is shining*
> *A leopard is giving birth,*
> *It's giving birth on a rock,*
> *Bombaibo, bombaibo.*

They pranced about as they sang, zig-zagging along the road. Then one of them said as loud as he could: 'Mpfffff!' Joe was frightened they might use the wrong word, so he cut in quickly with: 'It is the weed that drives away leo-pards.' All the other children broke out into derisive laughter. 'Leopard chasing weed, you do smell. Old squatting woman, leopard is afraid of your flower,' chanted a little girl whom Joe liked, dancing one step to the left and two to the right, and then bending down to touch the ground. Joe stood numbed. One of the big boys came to him, stood squarely in front of him and said, shaking his head from side to side, 'Tut, tut, tut'. Then he held Joe's chin in his big hand and said in a low but menacing voice: 'You do not call it that, boy. You call it sezimana, the vaginal weed.' Joe looked at him without reacting. 'Did you hear me, boy? Say it: the vaginal weed. Or are you too scared the Holy Ghost will rub munnyango leaves on your lips and make them swell?' All the children laughed except Joe. He could not say such a word. It was a sin. And tomorrow he had to serve mass, and if he served mass and did not have Holy Communion, the priest would be cross.

'Come on, boy, are you going to say it or not?'

Joe stood speechless, his tiny legs almost buckling at the knees.

'Well, are you?' The big boy made a big fist with his right hand and pushed it on to Joe's nose: 'Smell it and feel it; I call it the earth-mover. I split firewood with it and I dig yams with it. Now mind your ribs, or say it, boy.'

It came out before Joe could prevent it: 'Sezimana'.

He had not seen old Madalena approaching but she heard it. 'What shit did I hear come out of your mouth, Jojefu?'

'Nothing. I said nothing.' The other children began to move away furtively.

'Do you think my ears are mere mugs full of nothing but wax? I heard you say it, and now you insult my intelligence. By the uterus that mothered you, I'm going to make you pay for trying to teach all that filth to the young innocent girls . . .'

'I never taught anything to anybody, I was only trying to . . .'

'I am glad you didn't succeed. And stop interrupting me. I'm not your grandmother. Wait till I tell Mr Lizard your teacher. He'll make your anus spit fire,' she said waving her rosary beads in Joe's face.

It was no use protesting any more. The choices had changed. Now he would either have to run away from school or wear a lot of banana fibres under his pants to rob Mr Lizard's cane of its sting. What a mess! What a mess! He watched her go away, her cloth in her palm held firmly on her buttocks, and wobbling slightly.

Mr Lizard was the class master in standard three, and he had the longest cane in the school. Actually it was a scout-stave. He was a thin man with a gaunt face though, due to the loose-fitting Kanzu he always wore, nothing could be seen except his feet, which were very big. Their size was not necessarily the reason why he did not wear shoes. Maybe it happened the other way round; by walking, standing on, or otherwise exerting weight on his feet without putting them in containers to check their spread, he had caused them to grow too big. His heels stuck out backwards and were lacerated. His toes looked up almost as if they were deliberately avoiding the ground. They stood at right angles to the rest of his foot. Joe's grandmother said that Mr Lizard's toes were praying to God for rain in the dry season, and when the rains came they still stuck up in aversion to the muddy earth. Joe did not really believe this.

Anyway it was one of those mornings when everything seems to go wrong; when the sums don't come out right and you spill the ink in your copy book. Who should turn up but old Madalena. She told Mr Lizard her version of the story of the green weed. He was livid. His eyes narrowed and became red. He wiped his nose on the sleeve of his Kanzu and said: 'Joe, my son, it is hard to believe this of you, but I do.'

Joe tried in vain to explain that the whole thing was a mistake, and that he, Joe . . .

'Shut up and do not interrupt people when they are talking,' Mr Lizard growled, and Joe cringed back into his skin.

Madalena had done her damage by now and was disappearing down the road. The beast!

'Joe,' Mr Lizard said after a short silence, 'come here.' He sounded like a compassionate father who was going to give his son a manly talk. Joe went up to him, encouraged. Then, suddenly, Mr Lizard barked into his face: 'Joe, I'm not a young man, I was shitting in my pants long before your parents ever knew they were going to get together and give birth to a rat like you. Now I'm not going to have you spoil the good name of my class by shouting obscenities all over the roads in these villages. Lie down.'

Joe just stood there; he was not worried so much about lying down and getting caned; his mind was more worried by the fact that he could not somehow imagine Mr Lizard shitting in his pants.

'You and you there,' Mr Lizard pointed at two of the biggest boys in the class. 'Come and hold him.' Before Joe could know what was happening one boy held his two legs and the other his two arms and lifted him into a horizontal position in the air.

Mr Lizard got out the stave. He spat in both hands, rubbed them together to give them grip, then took the stave out of the armpit where he had been holding it. Perhaps he would not have hit him that hard. But the roof of the classroom was made of reeds tied together with fibres and there were lots of holes, so that when Mr Lizard raised the stave to hit Joe, its tip touched the roof, went through, and was stuck. Mr Lizard pulled and pulled at the stave, his eyes firmly fixed on to Joe's bottom where he expected the stave to land at any time. But as much as he pulled, the tip of the stave would not come out of the reeds. He stopped. All the pupils laughed and clapped wildly. Mr Lizard rolled up his sleeves, spat in the palms of his hands again, rubbed them together, and with great effort pulled the stave out. Joe was beginning to join in the mirth when the stave hit his buttocks. Once, twice, three times, he lost count. When they put him down again, he could not say he had buttocks at all. They were a piece of numb flesh stuck at the back of his front; he had no more claim to that than Mr Lizard. He walked back to his seat in the class, but he could not really sit down.

Later when he went home in the evening he was limping. What was he going to say to his grandmother? She would not believe his side of the story if he told her. Besides she was the one who told him never to let that word cross his lips.

'What happened to you, Jojefu. You are limping,' his grandmother said to him as he came towards the house.

'It's that boy Joni, granny.'

'And what did Joni do to my Jojefu?'

'He put a drawing-pin on my chair and I sat on it. My behind is very sore.'

'Oh, my Jojefu. If I could get my hands on the brute I

should make him call his ancestors from their graves. Never mind I'll boil some water and look after that.'

But this was only a temporary respite from the ordeal of owning up. In the end he would have to go to Father Balthazar for confession. And why did he have to ask so many questions? He did not have to know all those details to assess the gravity of the sin, especially when he had not even committed it. It was all right with Katende, the big boy with the yam-digging knuckles. He sinned and he liked shocking the priest. Anyway that was how it appeared, because after every confession he, Kiyonjo and the two boys who sold peanuts would get together in the middle of the playing-field or somewhere like that. Big Katende was always the one telling the stories, waving his left arm and moving his right hand up and down in his pocket. Joe would not have known what they were talking about if one day it had not rained ceaselessly and forced the boys to talk together in the classroom.

Big Katende had looked around before he started and had seen Joe at a desk at the back of the class. He paused as if to tell Joe to get out but looked at the rain outside. He shrugged his massive shoulders and bending forward he pulled the other boys with both his hands and said: 'First I told him I stole a duck from the rafter behind the Father's House and roasted it on a fire down in the Nuns' banana plantation. I paused to wait for the question but no flea bit my ear. Then I told him I had only attended part of the Mass last Sunday. He nodded his head. I suppose he saw the girls turn to look at me as I entered the church. But again no questions. I let a moment pass, and then said I loved a girl . . .'

37

All the other boys leaned forward and one of them said: 'And then what happened?'

'Don't pull my tongue; I am unwrapping what you are trying to open with your finger-nails.' The big boy was silent for a second, taunting their eagerness, then he said: 'He put his hand in his lap, drew his ear close to the small window and asked: "How?"'

'Did you tell him, did you?' they asked between each other's interruptions.

'Of course I did. That was the whole point, wasn't it?'

'You didn't!' the smallest of the boys said in disbelief.

Katende held him by the scruff of his neck, and shook him forward and backwards five times in quick time: 'I shall make a whistle out of your anus you bat-eared frog if you say I lie.' Then he let go of the small boy. He looked at the faces of the other boys to see if they doubted his story. If they had, it did not show on them. Katende pulled his shoulders back and expanded his chest: 'As I was saying, I told him I had slept with her; that's how I loved her. I swear I could hear his heart beat. Then he said "Did you sleep on top of her or sideways, or . . .?"'

'How do you sleep with a girl sideways?' one of the boys who sold peanuts asked, more in curiosity than disbelief.

'You are almost worse than the priest, you lot! Anyway I told him I had slept on top of her. So he asked me how far had I gone, and I told him as far as her backbone . . .'

'You do not go towards the backbone, you go up, into the stomach . . .'

'Look frog, don't teach me how to eat my yams. Stomach! Are you talking about a woman or a cow? In any case the priest believed it because he told me I had committed a very grave sin.'

'How many Hail Marys?'

'What was your punishment?'

'Three rosaries and as many masses over the next three days, boy, I . . .' The big boy turned round and saw Joe again. He looked worried. Walking up to Joe he held the front of his shirt and said: 'You can go and tell Lizard what you heard, but if you do, I'll . . .' Then Mr Lizard entered the room and all conversation stopped.

But Joe was still worried. He had been asked questions too, but nothing as drastic as that. Now suppose he went to the priest to confess that he told his grandmother a lie about the pin when in fact it was a beating which he had received for having been accused of saying something which he in fact did not say . . . 'Didn't you say the vaginal weed?' 'No, Father, I didn't say it.' 'Say what?' 'The v . . . the weed that chases away leopards.' 'What do you call it?' 'I don't call it anything.' 'Do you know what it looks like?' 'Yes Father, it's green and has yellow leaves, I mean flowers.' 'No, not the weed, you fool, I mean the . . .' 'Weed, sir? . . . er . . . I mean, Father.' 'No, boy. Now where does it grow?' 'In the elephant grass, Father. . . er I mean sir, sorry.' 'Elephant grass? What's wrong with the boy! Now listen, boy: is it hot or cold?' 'Lukewarm, sir, when the sun has been shining sir, Father, . . . er . . . I mean I don't know, sir.' 'Say it, son, come on say it, . . .' 'No I couldn't, Father, I couldn't. Old Madalena will report me to Mr Lizard, and then I'll limp, and have to lie to my grandmother and to come for confession . . .'

'Six times five is how much, Joe?' Joe had not realized

the arithmetic class had started. 'I repeat, Joe,' said Mr Lizard, 'six times five is how much?'

'It's green, sir, and has yellow leaves, I mean flowers, sir . . .'

'What's wrong with you, Joe?' It was the cold Mr Lizard; the scout stave could not be too far away.

'Nothing, sir.'

'Now stop thinking about that girl to whom you were teaching things, or you will never get anything into that head of yours.'

The whole class except Joe laughed hysterically to the gratification of Mr Lizard. He pulled his sleeves up to his elbows and twiddled his big toes. What the hell was wrong with everybody?

Many times Joe had longed for the day he would leave school, grow up and go into the world of adult pleasures. He had done so. Now here he was back at his school but as an outsider, looking on as a fugitive from behind a banana tree. He wanted to go back to this childhood. They would push them into the grass like that small boy, but he would not mind. He turned to Simon: 'Wouldn't you like to be young again. The world is cruel to men.'

But Simon preferred to be a man, grown up and fighting. 'I tried to, Simon; I tried to fight.' Then he seemed to swallow back the rest of the story. 'Simon, do you know Katende the big boy?' he said finally, and then added, 'of course you don't. But now, come to think of it, one of the soldiers who attacked me at the house reminded me of him very much. But I'm damned if Katende is in the army.'

Simon did not reply. He knew Joe was holding something

back. He had heard whispers and little conversations with the butcher the army had murdered. He could not tie it all up.

And Joe did not know how much he could tell Simon and still feel safe.

It had all started a long time ago, in Mr Lizard's class. Joe, Stephen, Matthew, Katende and another genial young man had struck up a kind of childhood companionship: the kind that survives on eternal petty intrigues and the ability to push each other into the grass without letting blood. First you get the bully on to your side by letting him copy the sums from your book. He never really gets to like you too much. For if you are like Joe, the budding saint, you are not much fun either. But the bully protects you, he survives on you. The other friends in the group take some of the pressure off your back. Anyway that's how it was; with Joe slightly to the fringe of the group and missing out on much of the conversation.

In Primary five, Katende began to falter, and his performance became worse every day. For one thing he had relied so much on being pulled out by his friends that he had lost much of the basic knowledge. For another, as he grew up, his interest in girls grew even faster and became an awful distraction as time passed. I mean when you are still young such interests tend to become all consuming and, well, a book is a book. At the end of Primary six, old Katende dropped out and joined the large herd of the lost youth. Three years later, Michael, the genial young man, failed his junior three examination and dropped out. Everybody missed him except the system. For the system is nobody's friend. All it has for you is a little hole. If it is square, so must you be; and if it is round well then you must also be. If you don't fit, to hell with you. I mean there are others to take your place. And who said the country owed you a living?

After that Michael tried a few professions without any success. He didn't really like what he was being pushed into. If you wanted to become a doctor you don't want to end up as a piddling veterinary assistant. You might as well go the whole hog and become a butcher. A butcher for God's sake! And that's what Michael eventually turned out to be. I wonder how he maintained his genial nature? Maybe to hide the bitterness inside him. A political time-bomb.

At Cambridge School Certificate, Joe got a first, Stephen a second and Matthew a third. In this country when you get a first, you can choose your career. With a second, you wait for lady luck. Get a third and you are in the dust-bin, unless, like Matthew, you happen to be particularly lucky.

And Matthew's luck was Independence. I mean you can't go very wrong with Africanization, can you? And while Joe and Stephen hankered after law and economics in England, with their newly-won scholarships, Matthew settled down to understudy one of the departing many in the Customs and Excise Department. He did well, and some time he was taken on one of those mashed potato courses at a Polytechnic in London. If nothing else, they give you confidence and power over your subordinates. Stephen read economics and returned to the Planning Unit in the Ministry. And Joe, well he just kept reading on and hanging around in England: law, economics and a lot more he gained by mere osmosis, rubbing shoulders and absorbing.

By the time Joe belatedly returned from England Matthew was high up in Customs and Excise, where Joe met him again when he went to claim his unaccompanied luggage. Joe began to shop around for a job but he had not known how to keep his mouth shut about his country's 'teething troubles' (as the liberals called them), and it appeared that luck was running out. It was then that he bumped into Stephen, economist at the Planning Unit. They talked at length. 'To hell with their jobs,' Joe said finally and he decided to strike out on his own.

Later the bitterness grew. The teething troubles looked like becoming endemic. But what can a man do about it? As Chinua Achebe once put it, you are like a dog trying to put out a bush-fire with his tiny fart. In the end, even a fart clears the conscience. So they bought a few guns. With Joe's money and Matthew's influence in Customs, this was not difficult. But what do you do with the damn things? I mean you cannot be expected to use them yourself. And who can you trust, to train? So all you can do is sit and wait, to contribute should anyone else start something. Soon, a creeping sense of disillusion set in, and it grew into a cancerous cynicism as they got older. In the end it appeared that only Joe who, not being a civil servant, could engage in trade, was the only one benefiting from the arrangement. The guns, safely stored at Michael's butcher shop, appeared to be destined to see only the blood of dead cattle. Dead blood, dead guns, and dead plans.

Looking back on it, the crunch must have come at one

meeting when Joe, overcome by academic interest of the problem, had explained that due to the tax structure of the neighbouring state, a man who could import and dump beef would become one of the richest men in Adnagu. For part of Joe's enterprises was a string of butcheries. He made a few suggestions. At the time he did not suspect what was going on in the minds of Stephen and Matthew. They knew Joe only too well and, later they had their own secret meeting.

'Well, I don't see why not. After all Joe is doing very well for himself. And you and I are stuck in the civil service till the *coup* comes – if it ever comes,' Stephen said.

'You know, Stephen, I'm beginning to think we'll all die civil servants and Joe will be the only man to have benefited.'

'I don't think I have the intention of ever letting that happen,' said Stephen, and he began to lay the plan for the importation of beef.

Joe knew nothing of this, till he discovered that they were in fact using his butcheries as outlets. For a long time there was argument and conflict between them.

Stephen argued, 'I don't understand your objection, Joe. After all I steal information from my Ministry, which is not right. Matthew here gets the guns through Customs, which is not right. And you agree with all this. But when it comes to us getting meat through Customs and selling it for profit you object. Why?'

'I'm afraid you're confusing your values. The guns are for a service to society. The information enables this group to make money to carry out that purpose.'

44

'Is that right, Joe? We sell our meat cheaper than everyone in this country. Isn't that a service to society?'

'Don't try to be awkward. If we don't discontinue this thing, we might as well disband. For we shall never be different from all those people we are trying to replace. Never.'

'Never? Well, are we anyway?'

'I don't know about you any more, but I am. Smuggling meat is not exactly my way of fighting a revolution.'

'You know what, Joe? You only say that because we sell cheap meat to your competitors . . .'

'My competitors. You own the majority share in this company, don't you?'

'Only because when we started it, you people hadn't enough money to subscribe for more than you got, and . . .'

'Well we are trying to make some money now . . .'

'. . . and anyway I pay my share to the group as well as everyone.'

'And who has the biggest pocket when we've all paid into the group? All right, Joe; I'll make you a proposition; let us redistribute the shares. We now have the money to . . .'

'You mean you now have stolen the money through your beef smuggling.'

'Whatever you like to call it; but we want to redistribute the shares.'

'No you don't; they're my shares and anyway I don't think I trust you any more.'

'I told you, Stephen,' said Matthew, who had been silent up to now. 'It's no use talking to him. He's too much in love with the money now.'

'Shit, man! You can have the bloody money if you like.'

'Well let's redistribute it then,' Stephen pressed again.

'That's not what I meant,' said Joe quickly.

'I told you so; I'm pulling out.'

'Pulling out? Are you two mad or something? All right; we've been planning this for years now. And now we have the guns, we have the money and all we need . . .'

'You have the money you mean . . .'

'All right. O.K. You pull out and what happens to the guns?'

'We sell them to the rebels in Anyek. Matthew can arrange the Customs end of the matter.'

'I am speechless. Honest, I am speechless. We spend seven years collecting guns for a revolution. And now we want to sell them because you men want to smuggle meat and get rich like every stinking . . .'

'Well you are rich and, if I may say so, you don't stink. Unless there is something wrong with my nose, that is.'

'Drop the nonsense, Stephen. I never thought we should come to this. All right. You can pull out. But the group stays and I keep the guns.'

'You must be joking, Joe. We sell the guns, or we stay in the group. But in that case you have to get out of it.'

'Me out of the group? Listen, this is too much. I'm going home. If you want me, telephone me. I'm disgusted with this whole conversation.' Joe grabbed his briefcase and tore out of the room.

The animosities which followed turned Joe in upon himself; he became a detached cynical man, who, with his riches, acquired with a different aim, must now appear as one of the worst exploiters in the country. Deep inside, however, he was an agonized man whose psychological breakup even sent him to see a witch doctor. Later, he had made a new plan with Michael, the butcher.

Now today, as he thought of the whole thing, he realized that, in fact that must have been it. Maybe now he was wrong and he certainly hoped he was. But something told him, with all the force of a sudden revelation, that in fact it was Stephen and Matthew who had organized the murder of the butcher and the raid on his own house, using the coup as their cover. They had all the motives. Besides, those men who had beaten up Joe were possibly not soldiers at all, just fakes, prophets in banana leaves, and their leader really must have been Katende, the boy with the big knuckles. Joe turned to Simon as they stood at the mission school watching the last of the young children go home. But he realized that Simon had not seen the raiders in the house, and that he did not know Katende, so it was useless to seek corroboration from him. He just let his hand drop to his thigh and with a frown on his face, wrote with his finger: 'First I will recompense their iniquity and their sin double; because they have filled my land, they have filled mine inheritance with the carcasses of their detestable and abominable things (Jeremiah 16: 18).' But his anger was confined to these scheming men who had been his friends. For though with every minute that passed he hated more and more the running away, he still saw no salvation in the city and no wisdom in fighting there.

The mission drum sounded again and there was singing and praying from the big church which stood overshadowing the school buildings. Unsettled by the frown on Joe's face Simon said: 'We'd better get going again. Mother is waiting at the house.'

The frown dissolved and Joe walked off feeling a slight relief. They were on the last lap of the long journey. Down the hill from the mission across the river and up another hill. Then they would turn a corner, and there to greet them would be his mother. Why can't it be like that always? To come without being pushed, and arrive to be greeted? But that is not the way things happened. 'At the beginning,' he noted, 'the mind sets out in mystery.'

They were both thus silently walking when a rat emerged from the grass by the side of the road. They stopped in their tracks as they gazed at it. It stood on its hind legs for a moment as if attempting an explanation of its presence. They watched it wipe its whiskers with its paws. Nothing new but something, some unexplained fascination, held them fixed. They waited, holding their breath and feeling slowly overcome by the urge to chase. Then, at some unheard signal, they pounced and ran after it. But the rat got away.

'Joe?'

'Yes, Simon.'

'What would we have done with that rat if we had caught it?'

'I don't know. I mean, how should I know? I've never caught a rat before.'

'But think, Joe. Think. If we'd caught it, what would we have done with it?'

'I told you I didn't . . . well we should have left it on the road or killed it and taken it to my mother's cat.'

'But cats don't eat dead rats. Not if they don't kill them themselves.'

'Well then we'd have left it on the road.'

'That would have been a terrible waste; wanton destruction.'

'A terrible waste of what? Nobody eats rat's meat; only the cats and they want to kill the bloody things themselves. I mean if I were a cat and . . .'

'But you aren't answering my question. If we had caught the rat . . .'

'All right, all right. We haven't caught it, so what's the problem?'

'The problem is, suppose we had caught it, what would . . .?'

'We didn't catch it, and I wasn't trying to catch it anyway.'

'So why were we chasing it? Why, Joe?'

'Well you chased it too. You tell me.'

'I don't know. I'm asking you.'

'Simon, I thought you believed there were certain things we couldn't know or explain – that we just do, fear and believe. That's why you've been getting out of the paths of ghosts all the time we've been on this road.'

'Yes, that's right, Joe. But you've walked straight all along as if you didn't fear or believe in things you didn't see. You must have reason for everything. So I'm asking you, if we had . . .'

'Do you eat rats where you come from, Simon?'

'No, we don't. Why?'

'Then why are you so disappointed we didn't catch the rat?'

'I never said I was disappointed. I just wanted to know why we ran after the rat.'

'Well, if you must know, Simon, I ran after that rat because it ran.'

'Because it ran?'

'That's right; because it ran.'

'And you, Joe, run after things that run, without any more reason than that?'

'What do you mean, without any other reason? Isn't that reason enough.'

'Reason?'

'Yes, Simon, reason. It isn't as haphazard an act as you might think. The causes are there in the unconscious mind, which also has its reasons. I don't know them of course. They dictate action and I perform; but I'm only a mere spectator to my own actions. I can't explain them to you because I'm not aware of the nature of their promptings.'

'I thought, Joe, you only believed in what you could verify.'

'I can verify the unconscious.'

'But not its reasons. Suppose I tell you that the real reason why we ran after that rat was that we both wanted to eat it.'

'Wrong. I'm not hungry. Things get chased because they run. As simple as that. Kayumba the cowhand once told me that the best way to fight a lion was to stand and look it straight in its face. It always runs away. But if you encounter it and run, you might as well put salt and pepper on yourself, to improve your flavour.'

'A lion with a belly full of antelopes, you mean.'

'No, any lion, Simon; any lion.' As he spoke the rodent

appeared again and Joe shivered out of the effort to control the impulse to chase. But he gave way and began to run. Simon grabbed him and they both fell to the ground panting. Joe noted with his finger quickly: 'I am sure there is more in a rat than I can see.'

In chasing the rat they had covered more ground than they had realized. As they got up they saw the house. Joe put his hand around Simon's shoulder, his heart burning with the excitement: 'Do you see that, Simon, do you? That's where I was born. And the woman is in that house. We are home. And this time I shall go further into the womb. I shall take the umbilical cord and tie it on my navel. Then I shall ask my mother to pull at it gently till I return to where I came from. I shall be safe there. Nothing will touch me there.' As Simon listened Joe noted: 'At last the mystery dissolves, and the will resolves. Liberty with the chance to choose again.'

'Mother!' Joe shouted, completely overcome; he dashed towards the house with arms outstretched, closely followed by Simon.

'Mother,' he called out again as he reached the courtyard 'We've arrived. Your children have arrived.'

There was no reply. That was not unusual. She probably was down in the banana plantation and her grandchildren had not yet arrived home from school.

'Mother, mother!' The chickens cackled in fright and hid further under the banana leaves.

'That's strange,' Joe said, fear and worry slowly creeping up his throat. 'Still we could hardly expect her to be waiting. She had no warning we were coming.' Deep down he knew he was only trying to reassure himself.

'Mother,' and the voice began to break under the weight of suppressed emotion.

'Why don't we take a look in the house, maybe . . .?'

'No, no, she'll come,' Joe cut Simon short.

'Why?'

'Why? Because she'll come, that's all. She'll come. Maybe she went to see the neighbours. You can't hear a voice call across the banana planations.'

'Mother, I know you're there. Come and greet us, we . . .' He stopped as he saw the marks of a truck tyre. Still he would not admit the possibility. But a tear betrayed him. 'Mama, Mama,' he broke down and cried.

Simon took him by the hand and led him to the house. 'Pull yourself together, Joe. Let's have a look in the house.' Together they walked silently through the door.

She sat there staring. The young girls lay in the sitting-room silent for ever. 'Don't come near me,' she said, 'I'm ashamed to explain to you, my son.' She was not crying. She just sat and stared.

Joe and Simon had stopped. What could they do or say? There was a vacuum and everybody was choking in it. Silence. No hens cackled. No cocks crowed. Just silence for the dead and the living, violated beyond repair.

Joe and Simon sat down and stared with her. Then suddenly as if by design, they all broke out and cried loudly, their bodies writhing and Joe banging his head against the wall. They cried for a long time.

When they had stopped and wiped the tears from their eyes, she greeted them. 'How is the town?'

'Bad.'

'Why do they do it, my son, why do they do it?'

'Mother, I once had a theory about these things. But no one can theorize about things like these. I don't know. I just don't know why.' Again they fell silent. Joe looked at his mother, and then the dead children. They were silent too but who could tell what they were thinking? Do the dead think? Maybe. Sometimes everything is questioned.

He thought to himself: I wonder what my mother, is thinking now. What do you think when you have been raped and you have just told your son about it? Why is she so quiet? Five hundred rifles at the butcher's shop; if each one killed twelve soldiers, that would be six thousand soldiers. But there are only five thousand in the army. I suppose we could take in a few civilians as well. Only where are the five hundred index fingers to pull the triggers? But I can try, by God I can. Then he noted down on his thigh: 'At what instant I shall speak concerning a nation and concerning a kingdom, to pluck up and pull down to destroy it . . . And I will make this city desolate and an hissing; everyone that passeth thereby shall be astonished and hiss because of all the plagues thereof . . . And I will cause them to eat the flesh of their daughters, and they shall eat everyone the flesh of his friend, in the siege and straitness wherewith their enemies, and they shall seek their lives, shall straiten them.' And in brackets he wrote: (Jeremiah – again 18: 7 and 19: 8 & 9. A very sore prophet).

Christ, everybody is so quiet!

'Well would you like some food, children?' his mother said finally.

'No, not for me.' 'Me none,' Simon and Joe replied together. The idea of food at a time like that. She was still a mother, raped, but a mother. And what mother can look at her children and not want to feed them.

'I would like to tell you how it happened. But I am too ashamed. I do not want to talk about it. How shall I stand among other women feeling the way I do?'

Joe wanted to tell her it was not her fault. But how was he going to say that? It sounded so hollow. 'I shall tie the umbilical cord on my navel and ask my mother to pull gently till I return to where I came from,' Joe had said only a while ago.

'We'll have to tell the relatives and neighbours. And God the parents of these poor things.' He looked at the bodies, limp and motionless. 'How does one break news like this?'

His mother did not reply.

Simon's mind seemed to be feeding on the anger of events which had overtaken his own family not so many years ago. In his heart he swore he would get the bastards.

'Well, my son Joseph,' she said. 'You arrange to spread the news. I'll stay here and await the arrival of the mourners. Besides I don't think I can walk properly.' She cried again, first for herself, and then for the dead children.

'Mother, I think I'll have to tell Uncle Yoanna and the others. They'll spread the news.' He was silent, but then added gravely, 'I have to go back to the city.'

'You must what? My child do you want me to lose even that little I've left to me. You can't leave here now. You must stay. Besides, how can you absent yourself from the funeral of so many of your children? Simon, tell your friend he mustn't leave his mother here alone, at a moment like this. I need help.'

54

Simon looked at her and he was seeing his mother. He said not a word. He just gazed ahead of him and listened to her voice. 'Simon, my son; they've finished me, they've finished me. But you mustn't let them get away with it. They've torn the flesh and beaten the brain to a pulp; and my soul has been left for ever to wander along the paths of insanity. You must catch them.' But Simon had done nothing of the kind; he had got a job as a servant and had forgotten all about avenging the fate of his father. He hated himself.

'Joe, where do you want to go?'

'I want to get back to the city, Simon. I must find out who did this or I'll go mad. Simon explain that to my mother.'

Simon knew the feeling too well. 'Mother, Joe will hate himself if he doesn't do what he says he must do. I know it too well.' But the mother only wondered what Simon was hinting at.

'But you can't go. It's not done. You don't leave dead bodies in the sitting-room and go off to town because if you didn't leave you would go mad. People would think you were mad anyway.'

'The people? Which people? And where are all the neighbours now? Where is Victoria? And her husband? The only thing they knew was how to come here bouncing their pot-bellies whenever they smelled the fat of roast meat hitting the embers in the fireplace. And where are all the rest?'

'Perhaps they would have come but the sound of guns kept them away. People are very wary these days.' His mother did not want to believe that it had come to that:

that in periods of danger, neighbours who come to eat would hide their heads under the dry grass in their sitting-rooms and let their neighbours die at the hands of strangers.

But these things had happened, and Joe knew it well. As for the reasons, no one could really tell. Joe had his suspicions. In the villages anyway, he felt, the old spirit of 'neighbourly brotherhood' was dying. It only remained in the mouths of the politicians in the cities who wished to justify their half-baked theories. As for the educated, that spirit had died a long time ago and the severe individualism of Europe had taken over. However, the sense of insecurity among the *élite* and their eagerness for fast material progress had produced a brand of young men, who though in a sense quite educated, lacked any intellectual commitment to causes. They thereafter became useless as agents of social change and progress since, to the insecure, any change to the *status quo* is considered a threat. They also became manœuvrable by those who had little respect for justice and other such nebulous principles of social intercourse. It so happened that those who had the vigour to manœuvre and change, were the chip-on-the-shoulder, beggar-my-neighbour, dog-in-the-manger little fellows who could not be adequately described by any number of clichés. They were, Joe felt, dishonest in motivation, crude in methods and ruthless in execution. They always won. But why did they win? Joe felt the argument with himself coming closer home. Why did they win? Was it not because the few young men who possessed enough sense to see the truth behind the pretensions – the young men who had been committed at some stage or other – had allowed themselves to be defeated by the apparent futility of all efforts at redemption? That they then escape into an intellectually respectable cynicism. And then with the proper amount of humour, suitably dehydrated, they turned their cynicism into a weapon to defend their comfortable detached existence. But is this not a betrayal of values as well? A betrayal even more vicious than straightforward cowardice and vindictiveness. In fact a betrayal so vicious that only the ruthless mind of an intellectual could stand it through its ability to cerebrate, detach, analyse and explain? Joe found himself asking: isn't this me? Me and the comfortable sofa and music. Me and the escape to the country home. Me and the money. But that could not be. He thought how he always felt strongly about things, but he could not move a mountain alone. Then it struck him that maybe everybody else he despised had come to the same conclusion by various ways. This world would never come to anything but a splendid mass of ruins; the archaeological evidence that man once lived here. That was difficult to believe. It could not be like that. He was only again trying to escape his responsibility. If only he, and other people like him, would exert their weight in public affairs then there would not be so much room for the triumph of the mediocre. He knew it. It was his fault. If only he and the others had acted in time the tragedy to his family might never have happened. Now he was feeling that he was really responsible. 'It's my fault, mother, it's my fault.'

'What fault?'

'It's my fault, mother, I should've stopped these men before they ever got into the position to come here at all.'

'I don't understand what you're talking about, son. How can one man and his friend stop a whole army with guns?'

'It's my fault, mother. It's my fault.'

'Now stop it, Joseph, and don't go on depressing yourself. No son of mine had anything to do with this.'

'Eh, mother,' Simon cut in. 'We have had a very hard and difficult journey here, and Joe hasn't been feeling very well on the road out there. But . . .'

'Nonsense, I'm feeling very well. I can see it all now. I can see where my proper responsibilities lie. I can no longer be deceived or deceive myself. Music, money, cars, brandy, it's all nonsense when we don't embrace it with the frankness of the shadows. I know now. They told me. Even what I see now gives me proof that I am right in what I think.'

'See what I told you, mother?' Simon was beginning to say.

'What have they done to my son? They have poisoned him. Look! The grief had blinded my eyes to what sat in front of me. How did you come? Where is the car? Let me look at you. Did you pass the night in the bush? You look so strange.' She looked at them, but Joe seemed to have his mind on things far from where he stood. She turned to Simon, her face plaintive. Simon told her how they had travelled from the city. But he did not know enough to tell her what had happened in the night that preceded the long journey.

But even as he told this story, Joe began to behave like a man possessed. 'Well then I must go and own up to the shadows, mustn't I? It's a cleansing,' Joe said with an intense terrifying voice.

58

'Sit down, my son. I will limber up to Anzera's house and get some medicine. Grief plays tricks with the minds of men. What are you going to own up for? You haven't done anything. You are not a soldier, are you? Answer me, son.'

'Me? A soldier? No, I'm not. How could I be?'

'Then what are you talking about? You're lying to me. If you did this to me . . .'

'I didn't, mother. Only I saw the shadows. And if you had been to see them, you would want to own up.'

'Me, own up?'

'Yes, mother.'

'God help me, he has gone mad.'

'Shall I bring a rope and secure him while you bring the medicine,' Simon said, vexed.

'Watch what you say, Simon,' said Joe. 'You may find that there's more sanity beyond the reaches of reason. For in their place there's no reasoned escape. There are only facts and their shadows. But before you have been pushed through the gap beyond the hills I cannot properly explain it to you.'

'Stay away from him, mother, I'll get a rope.'

'No, I'm not mad. Rest your minds. I only see where the naked eye cannot see; and there is a language there, and lots of toilet seats.'

Simon was now looking all around the room for some kind of help, though he could not really tell what kind of help. He remembered vaguely something he had heard Joe and a visitor discuss; something about curing the mind by going far back in time. One must go right back, he thought, to where the whole trouble started. He knew no more about the process, but he would try it: 'Boss, boss, it's me, Simon, your servant. Shall I fetch you some brandy? Your glass is empty.'

The mother looked at Simon and began to back away from him: 'Not you too. God help me.'

'No, I'm not mad. I'm trying to cure him. I'm his servant. I'm taking him back in time. Artificial inspiration.'

'God Almighty, now who will fetch the rope?'

'Boss, boss, it's me, your servant Simon,' Simon took a basket and was pretending to Joe that it was a tray of drinks, 'Will you have ice with it, boss?'

Joe stopped and looked at him as if he had not noticed him before. He followed him with his eyes: 'Stop it, Simon, now come on, stop it,' Joe ordered. The basket fell from Simon's hand. He stopped. Joe turned to his mother and said: 'Mother, I have no desire to go back to town. Only I must. I must. I can stay here to bury the dead. But that will not mean I won't be called upon again to do the same task another time. The solution is not here in the funeral. It is there where death originates; where power is misused. The misfortunes of my family demand a duty of me, and my honour demands of me the same duty; to return to the city and fight. And if the safety of my life should turn out to be the obstacle in my path, then my life'll have to go. We must change things or die.'

'Now you know, son, if you go there and get yourself killed I'll die too.'

'They cannot kill me. I shall live on, in honour.'

'Is this your honour the only thing that matters to you, son? These children here are dead, and nothing can wipe out what they have done to me. You think you will be happy to leave me here and go to get this your honour?'

'I'll come back, mother. I'll come back. Before the funerals begin. But I must catch Stephen and Matthew before they escape. If I can find that Katende thug, I have a good chance.'

'I don't understand what you are talking about. I don't know these friends of yours. But I have never known a son who left a mother to bury the dead because his honour is in the city where he must fight.'

'It's not like that, mother. The crimes committed against you must be avenged or, better still, prevented. If I went back now I could do both these things. Give me your blessing.'

The mother looked at the two men, perplexed. She felt her past, her present and her future knotted into one painful lump in her belly. Was the end near? Would she at last be released from this misery? The young must fight their own battles, wiping out the hope of the past. Then she looked away again and asked without expecting an answer: 'What blessing?'

Joe and Simon looked at each other. They had no alternative. They mustered comforting words to the agonized soul of the woman sitting there. They would return, everything was going to be all right. But they knew she did not really believe that. Getting up, they withdrew slowly from her presence and prepared to face the long road again. They would have to trace the story from where it began, and bring the culprits to justice.

3 It had been a normal evening as Joe returned from work. Simon opened the door for him and prepared the evening meal. After the meal Joe went to the sitting-room and sat on his emerald-green velvet sofa. It was a Tuesday so he switched on the radio to hear the jazz programme. In the years of seclusion and estrangement from society, after the break with Matthew and Stephen, he had come to like this programme which was a change from the endless platitudes of political speeches. The radio played Monk. Solid little notes cascaded and dropped like mercurial ejaculations out of the radio on to Joe's lap. Soon he felt himself sinking slowly into sleep until he could not really tell if he was thinking or dreaming. Suddenly the music stopped. It sounded as if it was the end of a song. But there was more to it. It was as if somebody had gathered the mercurial drops of the piano, squeezed them in the palm of his hand and thrown them back into the sound-box. Then there was silence; the kind of silence that signified not so much an end to something, more a beginning to some other things. An ominous silence.

Joe jerked himself up in his sofa and stared straight at the radio set as if expecting something to emerge out of it: an announcement, or perhaps more likely, an apparition. Maybe one of these pediculous politicians was going to put in a personal appearance in Joe's own sitting-room. Or maybe nothing was going to happen. He waited only an instant. The rich husky guttural voice broke the silence, in what seemed like a cross between an African Chief and a

British lieutenant right out of the passing-out parade at Sandhurst. He knew the words; even before they were spat out: 'This is the voice of the people of ADNAGU.'

'Here we go again.' Joe's reaction was almost ready-made. He thought. I knew it. Too good to last. It wasn't much, but anyway it couldn't last. Nothing lasts. Everything flashes across your consciousness and just as you try to touch it, takes its bow and begins to recede into the strange middle distance. Then other things appear to blur the picture, confuse you and disappoint you. Happiness and frustration jostle each other till everything becomes frustration.

Joe had heard too many voices of the people; and strangely enough they had all turned out to be the voices of a few individuals out for a kill. They impersonate you. Then they rob you and when you complain they laugh straight in your face. 'They couldn't have robbed you, because they are you, and how can you rob yourself? Come now, don't be ridiculous.' And it is then you feel like chanting: we are the hollow men, the hollow men, the owners of the means to production. Some of us live in the royal castles and others in the mud huts; but we are the owners of the means of production, the hollow men, the hollow men.

These thoughts flashed across Joe's mind as a single reflex without interrupting his listening. The wireless continued: 'The army has staged a *coup d'état* and taken over control of the Government of the state of Adnagu. All people are advised to remain calm and keep off the streets for the time being. A revolutionary council under Brigadier Okum has been formed and later he will inform you of its

63

plans. Please keep tuned to this station for further information.'

Joe permitted himself a smug smile. He had seen it and heard it all before. Was it going to be different this time? He would have to wait and see. His thoughts went back to the days when he was still a student of Economics in Europe. He used to think of himself as a well-informed young man. It was perhaps Europe's lack of knowledge of Africa which had made his own equally meagre information stand out above the ordinary, turning him into some kind of an expert. But it was more than that. As a student in Europe he had more often than not to defend Africa against all sorts of ridiculous arguments. This alone had forced him to inform himself about his continent. Though he did not consider himself an expert, he saw no reason to be worried whenever others took him for one. After all it helped his argument by giving it authority. It also greatly helped his own freedom from hunger campaign. Every *coup d'état* meant at least one TV appearance, one radio interview and at least a couple of newspaper articles. This, he had thought at the time, was pocket-money earned in a good cause; he used to give to his performances the dedication and devotional care normally reserved for a honeymoon. Now the freshness had turned sour, and if he were in Europe, and not so personally disgusted, he would get out his typewriter and knock out one for the daily newspaper, one for the women's magazines, and another for one of the other weeklies. He would phone up the television and radio studios and seven days later he would weep all the way to the bank.

Right now he could not be bothered. Anyway he had

made out well enough otherwise. It had been so wise to do law as well as economics. For, during the dull patches of 'revolutionary' change when his enterprises paid little, if anything, he had done well out of defending the 'criminals' of the out-going governments before they were shot. The failure of his legal defences did not affect his legal reputation because they were expected. Anyway there were not that many lawyers willing to take on these cases.

But first things first. Joe pulled himself out of his sofa as if he had suddenly realized he had been sitting there for too long. He must do something; within his own terms of course. Now what was his *coup d'état* drill? He had to secure all doors, switch off all the lights and change into his tough young revolutionary clothes. He then had to get out his car and make for the safety of his country home. He would return later for the legal hearings if he felt like it.

He prepared to leave. Then it struck him that maybe he should carry his gun with him. You could not rely on anybody at times like these. He put down his bags and entered the bedroom. It was under the pillow: two pounds of iron and wood. He loaded it and put it in his trouser pocket. Then he remembered his portable radio which he had almost left behind in his hurry to get away. He picked it from his bedside table and switched it on to check the batteries: '. . . stay at home'. It was the fag-end of the bulletin he had already heard. It continued: 'Soldiers still fighting in the Presidential Palace are advised to lay down their arms before they have their ears cut off. They are fighting a lost battle. The victory of the people of Adnagu cannot be reversed. People who must go out of their houses are strictly instructed not to carry upon their persons arms of any kind. Those caught carrying arms will have a chance to defend themselves before a military tribunal. Please stand by for further bulletins. The new régime salutes you.'

'Damn it,' Joe thought. Perhaps he ought to stay indoors this time. It was going to be safer there. He could just bolt the doors, have his gun near him, sit on his sofa and play some music. How about Mozart's *Requiem*. Poor devils! Dying out there in the streets. Can you die for anything any more? Maybe Stephen and Matthew would come into Government this time. Then it would not be safe for Joe. What can a man do when all that matters for most people is their self-interest? Joe's habit was to rattle off in all sorts of directions whenever he had an urgent decision to make; it delayed the moment of truth. Then he suddenly came to; a feeling of panic was overtaking him.

'What do I do?'

He positioned himself in front of the mirror and looked at himself. Tall, about six feet with his elevated shoes on and his hair grown high. He had never bothered to find out how tall he was without these. Anyway he spent so little time without his shoes and hair on that it would be pointless, at least in fighting terms, to find out how he looked without these. Looking at himself he felt impressed. A big man, and dark too. Maybe he could pass for one of those retired army officers and then he would be safe: one of the gang. But no, this was a time to use his brains, not his muscles, even as an aid to his brain. After all he had a pretty good brain and an opportunity to use it was always welcome.

66

He took the pistol out of his pocket and opened a drawer in which to put it. He could then move to the sitting-room, pour himself a drink, put some records on – not that blasted *Requiem* – think, and let the bloody fools waste their muscles out in the streets. The drawer stuck. He pulled and pulled. No luck. He would have tried another one but this was the safest drawer. It just had to come open. It was getting dark now and you never know who is watching through the windows. He must close the curtains first. In fact he could feel somebody watching him, from out there, peering at him through the window-pane with large red rolling eyes and an insane murderous sneer on the lips, ready to pounce on him the minute he turned his back. He did not need actually to see the fellow. It was this burning feeling he had on his neck whenever he felt he was being watched. He began to move towards the window. Then something, something nondescript, some moving object, propelled by a powerful agent, hit the window, made a messy spot on the window pane and fell away. It might be a locust or a grasshopper which in its blindness had hit the window at great speed, had burst, spread its guts around and then fallen away to make room for some other equally blind insect. They always did that. Well, it was either that or a murderous peeping-tom was spitting at Joe. Cheek! Good thing there were these winddow-panes or Joe might have got it straight in the face. Almost in a dive Joe grabbed and closed the curtains in one swoop.

He had shut the stupid world out and could now get along with thinking what to do. First he must put away that pistol. Bad piece of ironmongery, come to think of it.

Could not do much good. He tugged at the drawer without results. Then he stood back, held the knob, put his left foot on to the other compartment and pulled. The whole thing flew into his face scattering papers around the room. Joe spat, only slightly, inhibited as he was by the desire to keep his papers tidy. He went down on all-fours to gather the bits. He glanced at them briefly and popped them into the box as he went along; letters, documents and bills – paid of course. Then bang; there it was, right in front of him, staring at him, like the child of an adulterous affair it had charged him with its presence. He was its progenitor and now he had to possess it, awkward as this was at this time. He wished he could command it to disappear, dissolve and melt away into thin air, go for heaven's sake, cease to be. But no. There it was; solid, impertinent, staring and real.

He picked it up and held it in his hand: a document he had written in one of his enthusiastic moments. It was called: 'An inquiry into the methods of gaining and maintaining power.' It was modelled on Machiavelli's *Prince* and addressed to the leader of the Government which had just been deposed. It had been no more than a hilarious joke at the time he wrote it. But so much did it predict and echo the methods of the corrupt Government one might have thought they had used it as their handbook. Could he still explain it to the soldiers as a joke. They were known for their lack of a sense of humour. If he was caught with it he would be eating maize-meal in the local prison before you could say harambe. Something similar had happened to another brilliant young man fifteen to twenty years ago. He had been found guilty by association, detained and later tried. Joe could not actually recall the verdict, only the way people, especially Europeans, regretted the incident; they had pointed out how clever the man was, which did not cut any ice with the army, especially as most of them did not know whether All Souls was a strip club or some oil you used for your hair. Joe wondered what had happened to him. He must try and find out. But right now he must get rid of this document.

He was now talking to himself rather loudly. He wondered again whether in fact there was somebody at the window eavesdropping. Not that he had actually heard or seen anybody; it was just that feeling he always had; a seventh sense if you like. He could feel his words actually being pinched by some funnel-eared busybody. But this was ridiculous; yet the feeling was there as certainly as that document he held in his hand. Joe took hold of himself, stretched his body and slowly made for the window. He held his breath and put out his hand to grip the curtains. In one sudden pull they were open. Damn it, he had forgotten to switch the light off first. Now everyone out there could see him and right through him. A swift dive across the room and in a second the light was off. There now: he could see the street lights outside and the snoopers. That knee again: he always knocked it on things whenever he tried to hurry. Must be in the wrong place or something: perhaps too far down his leg, or too much out of line with his buttocks. Whatever it was it just could not go on, he would have to see a doctor before long; the way he would have to hurry in those coming days he might knock that knee right off his leg.

He approached the window and stuck his nose to it, the

better to see what went on outside. 'Haaaaaaaay!' The shout came out of him as if it had been squeezed out of a rubber doll. He felt the skin on his head grab his skull tighter as if to hold on to the hair which, he could have sworn, was flying off his head. He drew sharply behind the wall and held his breath. He could have sworn to the gods of heaven and earth that he saw a man approaching his house. In fact there were two men, perhaps more. They had guns, with fixed bayonets and grass on their heads. Camouflage they called it. They must either have been soldiers or madmen; not that it made much difference either way. They were crouching towards his house. When they saw his face in the window, they dived behind the rose bushes. Steady now. He must not get out his gun to defend himself. They would not understand. In fact he must hide that and that document and then sit in his chair, brandy glass in hand. Should they break the door and enter the house, he would confront them with such tranquillity and grace that they would be unable to harm him. Anyway he certainly was not going to hide in his wardrobe. That was no good. Another chap, a Prime Minister actually, had done it some twenty years ago and the damned soldiers had shot the shit out of him. Messed up his wardrobe as well. There is nothing like cowardice to attract violence. Look the devils straight in the face. That scares them. Damn it! Did you hear that? It was footsteps. What the hell did they want? Somebody must have been telling lies. No. They could not have come by that copy of the document he gave that girl for a laugh. Maybe they had. That girl, that girl, let me see: she went out with some unscrupulous minister. They could have taken his 'Methods' from her and the bloody revolutionaries might be searching for the author. Well he would just have to explain. He limbered back to his chair, got himself a brandy and sat there with all the dignified calm of a sphinx.

He began to feel very much shut in: imprisoned in his own house. The doors were bolted and there were soldiers all round the house. No good trying to get out. He would be shot 'trying to escape'. Makes good headlines that sort of thing. They would just have to come and get him. And he was sure that was what they wanted.

It is a strange feeling. First you lock yourself in. Then you begin to feel an irrepressible urge to get out. But you know you cannot get out because soldiers are waiting out there to shoot you for what crime you do not know. So you begin to feel an even more irrepressible urge to lock the whole lot out. And the more you secure the doors, the more incarcerated you feel. The more the outside world approaches your doors, and fiddles with them, the more claustrophobic you feel. It is as if you were expanding from within and generating heat, but at the same time trying to contain yourself and generating even more heat that way.

One sip of brandy, two sips, thr . . . he almost spat it out. That wasn't somebody knocking at the door to be let in. That was somebody trying to break in. Steady now; if you tremble you've had it. Then a chasm of silence; dark and unfathomable; you can actually hear the sound. Everything stops and no waves tickle your ear-drums; only inertia in the absence of movement presses upon your brain, relentlessly. A live kind of silence. Not just a gap between sounds but the zenith of sound. Not an interval in life, but a moment on the other side of life. Death must sound like that.

The silence was shattered by what must have been the butt of a gun cracking the front door. 'Holy smoke! C-c-c-c- coming,' Joe stammered as he made for the door.

He had only moved a few steps when the door burst open under the pressure of guns and bodies and five soldiers spilled into his house; tall dark uncompromising figures, on whose faces a smile would have looked like a crack in the battlements. They just stood there and stared at him, guns pointing and fingers tickling the triggers. Any minute now those guns were liable to burst out, and he would be on his way to eternity before you could say uhuru. One minute. Not a word. Maybe they were not real. Dark hallucinations come out of fear and two sips of brandy. They must dissolve away, out of his consciousness; come on, go away soldiers; shhhhh, tut, tut, tut, ksu, ksu, miao, miao; not a word, not a move. Joe broke out into a devilish laugh; he pranced about the house, scratching himself and laughing and muttering a freedom song all at the same time. He grabbed a side lamp from the coffee-table and legs apart he raised it above his head, facing the five soldiers. They looked at him, unmoving and unbelieving. His sanity, he must watch his sanity.

He returned the stony looks. 'Hurrah to these marble masterpieces of sculpture, drenched in the soot of the factories of human bondage. I shall drink to your dark regal beauty my inopportune visitors. You and I freeze into the monument to the unknown Simba of years ago.' He rolled his eyes and stuck them up into his eyebrows, and he was motionless. One soldier made as if to beat a cautious retreat from what seemed obviously a madman.

'Don't move,' commanded the sergeant. 'He's not mad. He's just trying to hide something.'

'Like intelligence for example,' said another soldier.

'Shut up,' retorted the sergeant. 'I aim to find out.'

'Where is he? Did you hear what I said: Where is he?'

No reply from Joe. He just stood there like the pillar of salt, eyes rolled up, with a macabre smile on his lips. 'I think he's dead, or possessed or both,' said another soldier barely hiding his fright.

'Shut up.'

Silence.

'Private, slap him on the cheeks, you know, like the nurses do in the hospitals. Come on.'

One of the soldiers made a cautious approach, slowly swaying from side to side as he did so; chwai, chwai, chwai, he rinsed both of Joe's cheeks.

Joe dropped the lamp from his hand. It shattered into small bits on the floor. Suddenly he woke up like a man rising from the ashes. He shook his head slightly and his eyes straightened. Then with an intense look in his eyes and crouching, he began to move slowly back away from the soldiers.

'Stop,' thundered the sergeant.

'What, what's going on?' Joe was beginning to come back to himself.

'Where is he, I asked you?'

'Where is who? I don't know what you are talking about.'

'Now don't you start thinking you can fool me, I'm not

as uneducated as some of you fellows think.' The sergeant accompanied his threat with a broad smile. He didn't look so bad when he smiled. About five of his upper front teeth were missing, which was a pity because those which had escaped the plucking by traditional custom sparkled white. His smile had an air of nudity which left Joe uncertain as to his own reaction; too broad a grin might be taken as derisive.

'I don't know what you are talking about, er . . . er . . .'

'Sergeant.'

'Er . . . se--r--geant.'

'Now where are you hiding him?'

'Hiding who?'

'The Minister for Civilization. We need him.'

'I'd say you do! Bad luck I can't let you have one; I haven't got him here. Anyway I've never heard of anyone by that title.'

'Private, explain what we mean.'

The soldier knowingly approached Joe and, without wincing, dug the butt of his gun into Joe's shin.

'Look here, what do you think you are doing? You can't do that sort of thing you know. We aren't living in the jungle,' Joe courageously protested.

'Something is wrong with him, sir. I hit him, and he knows I've hit him and he just stands there saying I can't do it,' said the private.

'I told you, sir,' another soldier volunteered. 'Them guys has been in school for too long. Had their brains washed. Scrubbed bone-clean. They don't even understand what power is. For them it's just words like, let me see, human rights and the dignity of man and . . .'

74

'Shut up. He's just trying to deceive us. Now where is the Minister?'

'Look, I don't know what the devil you are talking about. This is my house and I can assure you there is no Minister here.'

'You have no house . . .'

'Well, I say, aren't you being a trifle presumptuous?'

'I said you have no house. Now, corporal, you take the bedroom, and the rest of you take the other rooms and look for the Minister.'

'If I may ask an ignorant question, sergeant,' Joe said carefully. 'Don't you need a search warrant? Since not even a state of emergency has been declared.'

The sergeant suddenly came to attention, which made the other soldiers do the same. In a dignified voice he said: 'I hereby declare a state of emergency.' He paused and turning to Joe said derisively. 'Happy now?'

Joe stood there amazed both by the impertinence of the soldier and his own naïvety. The other soldiers disappeared into the bedrooms to look for the Minister. The sergeant walked slowly up to the curtains, pointed his sten-gun and suddenly pulled them apart. No Minister. He turned round with a smile on his face. The smile broadened as he caught sight of the tray of drinks on Joe's cocktail cabinet. He made for the tray and poured himself a large brandy.

'Hello,' Joe hailed with characteristic sarcasm. 'My name is Joe. We've been expecting you. Do come in. May I offer you a drink?' The sergeant wasn't amused. He stared at Joe over the top of the glass. 'Revolutions have a way of eating people,' he scowled. 'The wise only let it eat their property. Anyway I thought I told you you didn't have a house; now you don't even have any drinks.'

Joe looked on in silence as the sergeant drank a mouthful. 'Look, I'm sure you are either making a mistake or you don't know what you are talking about, which incidentally is also a mistake for a man in your position.'

'My position is quite safe and if I were you I would worry about your position, not mine.'

'I'm sure you would, but now that you aren't me, there is nothing very much you can do about it. Now I wish to tell you for the last time that this is my house and those are my drinks and if you don't get the hell out of here, I'm going to telephone my lawyer and the police. And I'll have you up for breaking and entering and for unlawful arrest as well. And that ought to settle your hash.' Joe seemed pleased with his own courage.

The sergeant just stood there unimpressed. At that moment the other soldiers emerged from the bedrooms, smartly came to attention and reported that no minister was to be found. The sergeant put his gun down and lazily settled himself on the sofa. He saw the cigarette box and opened it. It was a musical one and played 'Ave Maria'. He seemed quite pleased, as if he had played the song himself. He took a cigarette out of the box and offered some to the soldiers as well.

'But those are my cigarettes,' Joe protested.

'*Your* cigarettes, uh? So you think everything in this house is yours. Look, I've tried to explain: right now you don't own anything. Do you know something? I don't think you know what ownership means. I pour myself a drink and it's on its way to my stomach and you still claim it's yours. I'll tell you what ownership means: it means the possession of those things which you can continue to own against all claims of other people over those things. At this moment you can't stop us from drinking this brandy or smoking these cigarettes. You can't even stop us from taking that life which you still think is yours.' The sergeant made to pour himself another drink.

'I told you how very well educated the sergeant is,' said one of the soldiers nudging the other in the ribs.

'Yeah, I know too. I heard some guys say he went to some place in England called Sandhurst. They teach you real good there.'

'And you obviously went to Fort Laramie in 1860, or you've been watching too much television,' Joe said almost absentmindedly. 'Now, look here gentlemen. I respect your adoration of animal force, however unjustified it is by reason. But I think you ought to realize that there are limits to these things. Yes, all right, you are excited, and you come in here for some fun at my expense. I may even excuse that, within limits. But if you think you can come in here any time and deprive me of my privacy and possessions on some flimsy grounds, which I am sure you yourselves are far from understanding, simply because you happen to have guns in your hands, then I think this society has been foolish in letting men like you be the guardians of its peace. You have power, or at least so you believe, but you do not know what that power is for. Now I give you three minutes either to charge me formally of an offence or clear out of here. And I have a good mind to report you to your superior officers; drinking, smoking and stealing on duty!'

'One more word out of you and I'll show you what metal I'm made of,' shouted the sergeant.

Metal! It looks to me more like wood, Joe thought, but had not dared to articulate.

There was a tense silence. The sergeant moved over to the radio. He paused and then pressed a button. It played a Congolese cha-cha-cha. He put up the volume, and went back for his glass, which one of the other soldiers hastily refilled. He held it to his breast with both hands, half-closed his eyes, and danced with a shadow.

The soldiers giggled, grabbed their glasses and drank stiff doses. One took his gun and made believe it was his girl-friend. He held it in front of him and danced frenziedly with it. Two others slung the guns off their shoulders and then started to dance with one another. The other two positioned themselves at the cocktail cabinet and poured drinks. They just kept them going. Every time the sergeant turned to them he was handed a new glass which he empted, grimacing and then held it firmly to his breast. At every turn his eyes seemed to grow smaller and smaller. His steps became less steady as song followed song and the brandy flowed. The drops of sweat became more profuse and the stiff lips began to part slightly, revealing even less co-ordination. Joe stood there and watched his life go closer and closer to the precipice. Any minute now, any one of those soldiers was liable to pick up his gun and start shooting, at anything. It has happened before. It could happen now. It was certain to happen now. Look at those red eyes and those unsteady hands. If only they could drink themselves senseless, and do it swiftly. But they did not. They just stuck there in that dangerous mid-state, where the mind is terribly daring but the muscles have not yet weakened enough to deprive the bravery of all physical expression.

Then one of the soldiers turned to Joe and stopped right in front of his face. You could have lit his breath with a match. Ghastly fumes. He attempted to steady his body and smile, but his reflexes were almost gone and all he could manage was a macabre sneer. He struggled to lift his eyelids. But it seemed that each one of these efforts needed the total concentration of his whole body. When he tried to smile, his body swayed and his eyelids closed. Then he would try to steady his body, obviously the most urgent task, but this would leave his smile and eyes unattended. The smile would fade into a sinister half-dreaming threat and the eyes would close. He would then go for the eyes with a similar effect on the legs and lips. The struggle of man against the liquids. He wiped his mouth on his sleeve, and said to Joe: 'Don't just stand there staring, come and dance with us.'

'If you don't mind, please, I'm not quite up to it today. I've not been feeling well lately,' Joe said, characteristically.

'Hey, serge, he don't want to dance with us. He figures we's drunk.'

'Does he now? We'll see about that. Hey, Joe, dear boy, come dance this one with me,' the sergeant called out.

'You boys can go and enjoy yourselves, I . . .'

'Everybody sit down,' the sergeant thundered. All the soldiers scampered off to some chair. The sergeant sat on top of the cocktail cabinet. 'Now, Joe, you are going to dance whether you like it or not.' Joe was frozen; he could not think or react. 'Oh, yes, you are going to dance to the victory of the people over their imperialist lackeys and stooges.' Still Joe said nothing. 'Corporal, explain what I mean.' The corporal explained and Joe winced with pain. 'Now are you going to dance?' Joe said nothing. 'Now get on to that floor and dance.' Joe was shoved into the middle of the room. He looked about himself like a bashful, but anguished and confused bride, his face a mask, lamenting the freedom of yesterday. 'Dance.' The command pierced the free will like a sword and Joe began to contort to the music. 'I said dance, not wobble.'

The other soldiers giggled and pointed. Joe just went on wobbling to ward off the bullets. He could feel his spirit give way but he explained the whole thing as cleverness on his part; he would dance and the bloody fools will be amused and go away. Then tomorrow he would see his solicitor and then they would know all about it. If he did not dance, nobody, including himself, was likely to know what hit Joe.

'Stop,' the sergeant commanded. His face broke into a smile which revealed he was about to announce an unsavoury but, to him, terribly amusing happening. 'Now ladies and gentlemen, it is my great pleasure to introduce to you straight from the Follies in Paris, the world famous stripper, Joe the Stripper.'

He must be mad, Joe thought. This is the limit. Now I must die, a gentleman. The other soldiers gleefully applauded and waited for Joe to start his act. He just stood there like a Henry Moore sculpture, with holes through his body and soul.

'You are on, stripper, go on. We don't want to disappoint the customers, do we?'

Joe just stood and maintained a dignified but scared silence. Suddenly all the soldiers got up and gathered around Joe. They tugged at his trousers. He could feel his soul sink as they fell. Fight and die. If you do not you will never be able to face yourself again. Come on, fight. Hit one on the head and that will be that. Never mind that you have not drawn up your will. Never mind your life insurance. Suppose his friends ever got to know about Joe the Stripper? He would never be able to live it down. Come on. And then all of a sudden, that ominous silence again. They had all stopped in their tracks; two of the soldiers were holding Joe's trousers and the others had gripped his shirt.

The silence lasted for a minute, and then the voice came over the radio: 'This is the voice of the people of Adnugu. All resistance to the revolution has been broken and return to normality is promised as soon as possible. Citizens are warned that there are certain men masquerading as soldiers of the revolution and terrorizing the population. Anybody with information about these despicable elements out to spoil the good name of our country should report them immediately. All political prisoners . . .'

The sergeant nervously switched off the radio. Just then there was a knock at the door. 'Nobody move.' The sergeant cautiously switched off the light. Footsteps scampered away from the door. 'Now, corporal, keep the front door covered; the rest of you make for the back door. And as soon as we are out of here each of you is on his own. Now get cracking.' The sergeant made to move towards the back door. Then he suddenly turned round and faced

Joe; he walked up to him and gave him a here-today-gone-tomorrow rabbit punch.

Joe reeled and saw light in the darkness. He felt a kind of heaviness come over him and he sank to his knees and then fell on to the floor. The world receded from him and he became a vegetable. Maybe he was still alive. Maybe he was dead, and this heaviness, this impotence, this insensitivity was the feeling of death.

Whoever had been knocking at the door, must have given up when he saw the lights go off. After all Joe had come to hate visitors lately. And it would not have surprised anybody who knocked at his door and was refused entry.

At the back of the house, the intruders scattered in different directions. Three of the younger ones threw away their arms and fled down the street. They had to be careful of the real soldiers who might be met around the corners of buildings in the city. The 'sergeant' and the 'corporal' thought it better to hide in the back garden. And this was where Simon had met them later in the night.

4   When you come to think of it, anything can become a prison, even a garden. In the end, unless one comes out of hiding, the hiding-place itself grows walls and gates and barbed wire, and the fugitive is shut in.

So, the sergeant and the corporal squatted some distance

away from each other, in the garden at the back of Joe's house. But they had to get away soon, or else daylight would reveal them. Yet out in the streets and byways, there were soldiers and people. If they met the real soldiers out there during curfew hours, that would be their end. If they did not meet them but met the people in the by-ways, wearing those fake army uniforms, the people might, if they outnumbered them, set upon the two of them.

Suddenly, behind this rose bush where he squatted, the corporal realized how to escape. He would get rid of his army uniform and throw away the gun. Then he would pluck some dry banana leaves which, with the help of fibres he would tie around himself as a garment. Thus dressed he would try to make his way home passing himself off as a madman.

But the attempt to carry out this plan had landed him with another problem which grew more urgent by the minute. He had to act quickly. Fear and drink had combined to activate the corporal's bowels; and now his enforced squatting position and intention to take off his clothes threatened to give his feeling immediate expression. He had to find a way out. I suppose he could have visited Africa, as you might say, but every man had their own limits. I mean we all have to draw an unlikely line somewhere. In the meantime the corporal decided to stand up and reduce the pressure on his body. And as he did, his head rose above the rose bush and he sighted the 'boys' quarters where Joe's servant lived. That was it. He had to give it a try. So he bent slightly, dropped his gun, put his right hand in his trouser pocket and with his rear muscles fully tightened, he made for the sanctuary of Joe's servant's

83

toilet. He felt as he went much like these new jet aircraft with their gaping engines at the rear. Up the stairs on tip-toe, two-by-two and on to the banister which in these houses is outside the house. He tried the hall door and it opened. Slowly along the corridor, carefully, and there it was; with the door open. He entered and was just in time.

'Gosh, I shouldn't have done that! That blasted flush system must have woken up the whole neighbourhood. Didn't have a choice though. Quick!' Out of the toilet, streaking down the stairs three at a time, across the garden in a flash, and he dived behind the rose bush.

Hold your breath now; no don't cough, that is dangerous; turn round, slowly now, no shadows; and he was right. The light had gone on in Joe's servant's bedroom. He calmed down for a minute. Then in a hurry he tore the banana leaves off the stems, taking care not to make any noise. He slung them around his body, sized himself up, straightened his shoulders, and he was ready for his new character; a psychotic paranoid, believing himself to be the saviour of the world from the scourges of sin. In this confused state of things, with uncertainty and revolution on everybody's mind, that ought to see him home.

Simon, Joe's servant, tore out of his bedroom like a ram on heat. In a second he was standing in the middle of the garden, a torch in his hand flashing in all directions, calling out: 'Who goes there?' The sergeant squeezed as close to the rose bush as the thorns would let him; he raised his gun to his shoulder and took careful aim at Simon and was just about to fire when a move from the corporal saved him from the mistake. As Simon flashed his torch around, underneath the flower-bushes and all over the place, its light caught the corporal's hunched body, or as much as it as could be seen through the dry banana leaves. The corporal decided this was his moment of truth and glory, when he had to embark on his lie.

'Hold it there,' shouted Simon, his voice charged with fear, 'I'm pointing a gun at you, and if I let it cackle, it'll lay some hot eggs down your rotten thieving throat.'

'Amen, amen, I say to you – drop that gun.'

'Don't move,' Simon warned again.

'I come bearing the words of truth on my tired and agonized head. This house has divided itself against itself, and it shall crash on to the heads of those that do not heed the words of God. I saw a star rise in the east to chase the white clouds which blocked the warmth of the sun. I heard a hurricane build up in the womb of the earth where the Great Bear points its tail. And I spoke to the winds that blew the spears from the valleys into the elevated regions of the Milky Way. Then standing on the horizon of my dreams I saw the white clouds descend under the weight of the great oak tree and dissolve and disappear, chased by the hurricane. I plucked that glittering star and placed it on a pedestal for the adoration of all wise men. But that star let me down. It did not stay up there to light the sky when the revealed sun went to sleep. Instead it became a rhinoceros and fell into the gutter behind the house of the Eastern and Western Merchants Limited. And then one day it ran into my garden, ate my yams and stuck its unicorn into my saintly back.' The corporal's voice was sonorous and theatrical. And he stood there, the torch, like a spot-light, picking out his sombre face and his body

85

resplendent in banana leaves, casting an awe-inspiring silhouette against the star-studded sky.

'Who are you?' Simon inquired with the frightened but inspired expression of a faithful disciple brought face to face with his unknown master for the first time.

'I am the truth.'

'But you are mad.'

'I am the mad truth. I commune with the body and the spirit, but above all the spirit.' The corporal, his arms outstretched took two steps towards Simon, who stood motionless. He would have gone a few steps farther. But then he thought the servant might smell the brandy on his breath and then he would have to run for his life or work out a whole routine on weddings, miracles and good and bad wine – which was not a bad idea itself. Or was it? He would try anything once.

'Brother . . . er . . . er . . .'

'Simon,' the servant said, mesmerized.

'Brother Simon, salvation lies right in our own arms. The world is full of devils who will give you a stone and tell you it is bread for you to eat. If we persist we have the power to turn that stone into bread or, indeed, cast the devils themselves into eternal flames. They served us snakes instead of fish when we turned up for the wedding of the seven sisters. They gave us vinegar to drink and kept the wine for their own private feasts. And I saw lies served on a silver platter. I tried to catch them but I caught the air only. We must watch and pray, brother Simon, lest evil men in military clothes should descend and hover above the rose bushes preparing to lead us up the garden path and into the paths of sin.'

86

The sergeant, hiding behind a rose bush got jittery at the turn the corporal's sermon was taking. Maybe the corporal was playing some dirty trick on him and getting his own back for something or other. The thought of shooting the two of them crossed his mind, but the corporal began to speak again.

'My dear brother, where do you lay your tired head when the day's work is done?'

'There are my quarters across the garden.'

'And why aren't you slumbering at this hour before the sun returns with its chores?'

'Because somebody I don't know, some stranger, has been using my toilet.'

'Using your toilet, uh?'

'Yes.' And then, his eyes firmly on the corporal's eyes, 'It wasn't you, prophet, was it?'

'You blasphemous infidel, I come here to deliver the word and only the word of the one who has sent me; and I do not concern myself with such mundane affairs that seem to be your worry at the moment. And what was this fellow doing in your toilet then?'

'Writing the rude truth on the wall, I suppose.' Simon was putting up a battle against the power and magic of this strange man. There was such a ring of truth in what this man was saying. Yet Simon could not believe him altogether. Indeed he had heard of even stranger prophets choosing to make the strangest and unlikely entries into human intercourse. But surely this would be some legend. A prophet behind a flower bush whose first disciple was woken from his sleep by the flush system of his own toilet, pulled by some mysterious being. No, this was a madman, lost somewhere between here and eternity.

Simon had to get the truth out of this man, but before he could say a word, a machine-gun rattled, some two or three hundred yards away. He wondered whether they were the rest of his soldier friends.

Simon froze into stone as he listened to the echo of death bounce off the rocks in the valley. And the corporal, sensing what Simon thought turned to him and said: 'And the vultures came to feast, brother Simon, and the vultures came. They picked the meat off the metal and bones in the streets of death and went on their way. For the sins of man have consumed him and death is his constant companion. We must watch and pray, brother Simon, we must watch and pray, for the hour shall come by stealth.'

Simon stood in silence and looked at the gun in his hand. 'And they that live by the sword shall also die by the sword.' The corporal could exploit an instantaneous advantage. 'Lay down your arms, brethren, and pray. That sword you are holding shall pierce the flesh but miss the heart; for the heart can only be touched by the truth in the words of men.'

'God save our souls,' Simon called out.

'Pray, brother, pray.'

'God save us from the iniquities of this world.'

'Pray, brother, pray.'

'May our sins be forgiven, may our souls be cleansed.'

'Throw away that gun, brother, and your sins shall be forgiven.' Simon let the gun drop from his hand. The corporal smartly picked it up, feigning disdain at the same time. 'Peace be with you, brother, and may your hands never be soiled again with the instruments of death. And now, brother, kneel and pray.'

Simon sank to his knees, bent his head and held it in his hands. 'For the meek shall inherit the earth. Let the Lord possess your body and soul.' Simon bent till his head touched his knees, and was silent. And the corporal, testing the completeness of his lie, said: 'The dove came and perched on his shoulder, and a louse from his hair did it pluck.'

'Amen,' said Simon, completely possessed.

Slowly the corporal backed away; one step, two steps, faster and then he ran, the banana leaves on his body flying in the air like the wings of an eagle. He turned the corner and disappeared.

'Arise, brother, do not yield your head to the temptations of earthly slumber. For the thief came by night when the world was asleep and their souls did he steal. Rise and pray, brother, rise and pray.' Simon heard the voice from above his head and it was a different voice, big, booming and husky. An apparition? The Lord himself comes to take his own into his custody? Slowly Simon lifted his head to look to the sky and almost stuck his nose into the barrel of a machine-gun. For the sergeant had now got into the act. Simon moved his eyes up along the barrel of the gun to the uniform and to the belt, packed full of bullets. His eyes stopped. He made as if to scream but his throat was stiff and nothing came out except some kind of throttled noise, like the whisper of a crocodile. He just knelt there in front of the sergeant. Was he real or was the whole thing just a bad dream? Suddenly he realized that this whole thing was a trick and that he had been caught out;

now he must scream, surrender or die, or all three. Simon opened his mouth as if to scream.

'Shut up. One shout out of you and this squirrel here will bare his teeth.' The sergeant fondled his gun. 'Now, get up and get back up there where you came from.' Simon got up, his hands above his head and walked towards his quarters. He was followed by the sergeant – his gun pointing at Simon's back. They climbed up the stairs and went into his room. There the 'sergeant' bound and gagged him. Then he went outside, locked the door and threw away the key. That was half his problem solved. Now he had to face his wife. It must be about three o'clock in the morning, which would probably be four on her mental clock. He would have to have a very good excuse, but it was not going to be too easy all the same. The bitch!

He concealed the gun under his clothes and, avoiding all streets where he might be seen, made his cautious way home.

As he struggled around his room to untie himself, Simon shuddered to think what might have happened to Joe, his boss. He did not know who these men were or whether they had been inside Joe's house. Something inside him told him he had to get to the house as soon as he could. But he was not to succeed until the morning.

Meanwhile, inside the house on the floor, Joe lay motionless, pressed down by a kind of dead-weight heaviness. A pale darkness pervaded the room. He might have been able to discern a few objects, but his eyelashes were interlocked and he could not open his eyes. Suddenly he began to hear voices.

'I wonder if he's properly dead.'

'Why, do you want to eat him?'

'Shut up. Anyway it's better than feeding him to the trees and flowers in the cemetery. This world is mad, I tell you,' the older of the two voices continued. 'But it's not my fault, is it? I'm not after anybody's blood.'

'Blood, blood,' a female voice screamed from a bit farther away.

'Who spoke of blood? I'm a virgin, so leave me alone.'

'She is a bad case that one. I mean she ought to be fumigated, you know what I mean?'

'No . . .'

'Sshh . . . shut up, here they come.'

'Are we going to let them take him away?'

'Well it's not their fault, is it?'

Two men with long guns approached Joe's prostrate body. 'You must come with us to the cleansing,' one of them said, without threat or menace, just conveying information.

Joe shrunk away. He attempted to say something, but a thick glue filled his mouth. Yet, though his shrinking could not be seen and his voice was inaudible, the two men saw and heard. One of them said to the other knowingly: 'You see, I told you he wasn't properly dead.'

'But he must come with us all the same,' the other man with the gun replied. 'We're only the messengers of death, not its accomplices.'

They were just about to touch him when the older of the other two voices screamed out: 'Leave him alone. I said leave him alone. Now you all eat cabbages and onions and garlic, don't you?' There was a silence of agreement. 'So why pick on him?' But the men with guns simply shrugged their shoulders and began to lift Joe.

'You'll have his blood on your hands,' the younger of the voices intoned, trembling.

'Stop talking about blood, I said,' the woman screamed, 'I'm a vir . . .'

'Oh shut up . . . they can't take him, can they?'

'Joe, take your barkcloth and come with us, we must arrive before the cleansing,' the more officious of the two gunmen said.

'But he hasn't even got a barkcloth,' the other one observed.

'I told you he wasn't properly dead.'

'That's not our fault, is it? He must come with us all the same.'

The heaviness began to leave Joe and he felt himself floating upwards. His whole body floating into the air.

'They're taking him, the bastards,' the old man spat.

'Hey, what do cabbages and onions and garlic have to do with all this,' the young voice asked the older one.

'Are you stupid or something? It's the cleansing. The shadows. If death does not fit him for the cleansing, he'll become a whirlwind and he'll be sent back to us, like you and me, for ever to blow circles in the dust. It's an evil existence between the deceit of the humans and the frankness of the shadows. That's why men step out of our paths.'

As this conversation went on, Joe continued to ascend and his eyelashes began to unlock. Below him he saw a huge valley. Crowds of people could be seen. Some of them were wailing and calling him to come back. Others sang, led by a man in long robes who, from time to time, threw water and smoke at Joe's floating body. He drew farther away. When he turned to look ahead of him, he nearly crashed into the horizon. But the men with guns pointed at a spot on the horizon. A red gap opened. Joe was pushed in, and then all was floating, silent weightlessness.

'They're waiting,' one of the men said pointing at dark figures in the valley behind the horizon. They sat silently. As Joe descended and alighted, he noticed that they were shadows of men. They all sat on lavatory seats and they were taking notes on toilet paper. They appeared to be speaking in turns. Then suddenly they all stopped and looked at Joe. He did not know what to do or say. He only stared back at them. Was somebody going to offer him a seat, for God's sake? His legs were getting weak.

At that moment one of the shadows rose and began to speak. 'Your distinguished excellencies, ladies and gentlemen; we've all been pushed through the gap in the horizon. We've been all things to all men on the other side. Here, we're just shadows at the cleansing. We must declare the truth inside us. Truth is the concurrence of the interior and exterior of man. What we're about to do in testimony to our inner cleanliness, we ought to be able to repeat right on our thrones, in the streets and avenues that bear our names, in the pulpits and in our marital beds. The bond of the entire truth between men.'

As he stopped speaking, he returned to his lavatory seat. Another man appeared and led Joe to his seat. Then there was silence.

'He's holding his nose, damn it,' one of the shadows pointed at Joe.

'He's not properly dead; he can't embrace the frankness of the shadows.'

'He's a whirlwind.'

'No,' the man who had spoken said finally, 'he's not crossed the line. He'll have to go back and die properly. Confess to himself. Otherwise how can we tell him what we really are? He'll think, we're just a load of, well, testimony.' Then the shadows appeared to dissolve, though Joe wanted to hear more.

'Boss, boss!' More loud knocks on wood and then: 'Boss, boss!'

'Oh shut up, I want to hear more from the shadows.' Then music. 'Canned music even here for Chrissake.'

Loud knocks. 'Boss, are you in there? Open up.'

'What? The music has stopped?'

Three loud beeps and then a voice: 'Seven o'clock East African time. Welcome to your Breakfast Club sponsored by Andrew's Liver Salt.' Then music.

'Damn it, there isn't supposed to be any time here. Andrew's maybe . . .'

'Boss, I'll have to break in,' followed by a loud crack of wood.

The heaviness returned to Joe. Kaleidoscopes fluttered. His head was a block of ice encased in bone. He tried to get up but reeled and fell over before Simon could grab him. He stared at Simon for a moment. 'Where are the shadows,' Joe muttered. 'I want them to tell me some more.' And before Simon could interrupt he added: 'You won't understand, Simon. Come on. Help me up.'

Simon had made a bed for him, cleaned up and had then gone to the butcher's shop.

Now they had made the trip to his mother's home. But there was no refuge there. So they had to take the road back, to their responsibilities in the city.

5   The road back to the city is not taken lightly. But there Joe hoped somehow to bring Stephen and Matthew to admit to conspiring to murder the butcher. He would turn them in to the police. They might retaliate by revealing the details of the guns at the butcher's shop, but he would have to take care of that somehow.

First of all he had to find the men who raided his house. Every minute that passed made him more certain that the sergeant thug was none other than Katende. Then they might be lucky and have a clue in the form of a uniform which one of them would have left behind if, as Simon had said, he had seen a man dressed in banana leaves. If they could find the uniform, and maybe some documents in it, they would be able to trace at least two of the thugs, although Joe had in fact not seen Katende since they were at school together almost twenty years ago.

But in the time it had taken Joe and Simon to walk to their mother's home, other things had happened, and even before. Since Katende left school he had been caught by so many of the barriers in the way of his progress. Having always been a rebel he had got himself into one kind of trouble after another. Partly as a result of all this he had changed his name more than once. Katende always used one name at a time, Christian or surname. At the moment it was Yacobo. Joe and Simon did not know all this.

Joe's house stood on one of the hills on which the city was built. Between it and the mud houses on the plain below was a precipice created by the Italian constructors who had built the tarmac boulevards that criss-crossed this fashionable neighbourhood. One of the red mud houses below belonged to the sergeant who had raided Joe's house. His name was Yacobo, alias Katende.

At about three o'clock in the morning, Yacobo had locked Joe's servant into his little house, and was making now his apprehensive return to his own house and his wife. He slung his gun over his shoulder, sat on the precipice, and jumped to the lower level below; as he landed a searing pain went through his right ankle. He paused for a moment to absorb the pain, and then continued, cautiously, keeping his head to the ground and his eyes alert.

The small path through the slum village wound its agonizing way past windows, doors and kitchens. He could all but hear the snoring from inside the house. Then his foot slipped. He almost fell but regaining his balance he discovered that some drunk had only been shitting around the byways. He cleaned his shoe by rubbing it against the mud veranda of the nearest house. At last he rounded two little shacks and came face to face with his own house.

It stood like an overgrown hippopotamus in the nascent light of the stars. He did not like it. In fact he had always intended to go and live somewhere more respectable. Always something happened to prevent him keeping his promises to his wife to move out of this stinking place. A change of job maybe; he never seemed able to keep his jobs for long. Not that he totally lacked education. Far from it. All his former class-mates were now clerks in Indian offices in the city. But he could neither stand Indians, nor any other bossy small-time employers. It was bad enough to be ordered around. But if the order came floating on a stream of garlic breath, day in day out, that was more than any man could stand; unless of course he happened to be Indian himself.

Then there were the Italians who made roads. He had thought of them too and in fact went for an interview. Apart from the absence of garlic they were almost as bad, swearing at everyone and everything in sight. And those ridiculous mini-shorts they all wore, exposing their bums, raw from sitting too long on tractors and bull-dozers. Anyway they seemed uneducated themselves and all they knew was how to drink and to fornicate with the local girls.

As for the government; well, that would be nice but it always seemed so difficult to get work there. There was so much competition. Maybe he should have gone into politics and joined the youth wing. With his taste for violence he might have done quite well; that was difficult at his age, although some of the youth wingers he had seen were anything but youths, or wingers for that matter. Anyway it had been at that time that the Congo had happened. He had gone off there, as he put it, 'to gather what the fleeing Belgians were leaving behind, and save it from

97

going to waste'. The gun he wore on his shoulder was one of the less perishable commodities he had acquired there.

Now he stood again in front of this house. It pointed at him accusingly. The familiar feeling came again; a kind of abdominal emptiness like a childless kangaroo; the light emptiness of a heavy pouch of feeling. It rigidified, churned and moved upwards tending to make him bring up. That was the nearest he ever came to having a conscience. Perhaps that is what it was; returning from his stomach, where his nocturnal revelry had sent it, to the chest at the thought of his wife.

He knew she was sitting in there waiting for him. One look at him and she would see right through him. In fact that was what was wrong with her and the whole blasted marriage; he was always being forced to be himself. Who can live with reality every minute of the day? Is there a reality so embracing that it can be man's permanent and loved friend? And to personify reality is to attract to one's self the antipathy normally directed towards brutal facts. You become a brutal fact.

He arrived at the house and let himself in. He was right. She was there waiting. He faltered in explaining his recent whereabouts.

'Don't lie to me. I know you too well. I've lived with you for so many years. God knows how I've done it, but I've done it. Must be my stupidity or something.'

'I would agree with the stupidity bit . . .'

'All right, go on and abuse me when all I asked was where you have been all night. And I suppose that is something women never ask of their husbands?'

Rozalia, for that was her name, had a straight back. That is not all she had but it was what struck you when you saw her. At the top of this back, and just at the foot of her neck, two shoulders perched in conspicuous configuration. In between them, like a flag-pole, a neck reached out and held up a head. Running from her shoulders downwards and to the back were two arms, whose elbows stuck out like quills and gave the impression that she had been growing them for a long time. At the foot of her straight back, buttocks. They did not tremble and wiggle like other women's when she walked. It must have been due to the firm grip her back had on them. Her legs remained a matter for conjecture, eternally covered as they were by her long costumes.

She fixed Yacobo with that unnerving gaze. Her eyes, widely separated by a barely discernible nose-bridge, were small and piercing and her lips thin and set. 'Where have you been?'

'I told you and you said I was lying.'

'And so you were! A revolution! Fighting for the masses. You? You trembly trousered toad? Fighting for the country? Eh? What was it you did last time we went to the forest together and that snake rolled his eyes at you? Did you kill him? Did you strike him with that timid stick of yours? Of course not. You ran like the winds of Ddumbi and urinated on your toes.'

'I knew you couldn't tell the difference between killing a snake and fighting a revolution. Anyway who can fight a snake and a wife at the same time?'

'Now I know you are trying to do. You want to annoy me, so that I won't ask any more questions. But I tell you:

99

you can go and practise your cleverness on your jigger-toed friends. I'm not as stupid as I look. Now where have you been?'

'Haven't you heard? Or are those ears mere decorations to deceive the butchers you are not a cow?'

'I have been around for some time now but I've never heard a man talk like that to his own wife. It's a sign of the times. Is that what you learnt in the Congo, along with lifting things? Now listen to me: that head of yours is a calabash full of nothing but a cobra's tongue, cursed for ever to speak venomous spittle. Where, I repeat, have you been?'

'Woman, I only married you, I did not ask you to be my jailer. If you do not want to believe what I say, you can go and suck on the ashes in the fireplace to keep your mouth busy. But I have told you . . .'

'He, he, he, I'd sooner listen to a squirrel's fart. I've never met a man who lied so much in my whole life.'

'Watch your tongue, Rozalia, I'll not take that kind of rubbish from a woman I paid for.'

'You can go and get your miserable money back. I've given return more than your money can buy already. And if you don't know it, the witch that's sitting on the pots for you must be smoking a pipe a mile long. If I left you, you would starve to death. If, that is, they don't put you in jail first.'

'You can't threaten me, you know. If you want to go, why don't you go, and let's see how I die?'

'Because I should rather be the wife of a louse than its widow. Now, where've you been?'

'I told you. Now can't you see this uniform I am wearing?

There has been a revolution and I've been out there fighting for the masses. To help them . . .'

'Help them do what?'

'How should I know? I mean help them get rid of colonialism, imperialism and neo-colonialism.'

'I thought they got rid of that years ago.'

'Not exactly. You see the enemy keeps coming through the back door every time he is pushed through the front.'

'So you've been locking the back door, hi, hi, hi. Everybody should live in a hut like ours. No back door, no neo-colonialism sneaking in.' She laughed till the tears rolled down her cheeks, 'Is that why we've never moved from this hovel?'

This really got Yacobo on the raw, but he sniffed and straightened his back to look brave: 'Now look, we've been out there facing the bullets of the enemies of our society, and what do I get from my own wife? Scorn. How do you want me to prove the truth of what I am telling you? A wound in my ribs for you to stick your quill of an elbow in?'

'Now leave my elbows alone. They are better than your vestiges. Just tell me where you have been.'

'It's your fault. If only you had switched on your radio, you would have heard the . . .'

'Have you forgotten we ran out of batteries a month ago?'

'You mean that thieving bastard of a mechanic hasn't brought my batteries yet?'

'If you mean Zakariya, I met him only yesterday and he said he knew nothing of the batteries.'

'Thieving capitalist hyena. You didn't believe what he told you of course?'

'These days I don't know who is telling the truth and who is telling lies.'

'Thief!'

'He said something to the same effect about you, only I didn't want to mention it to you, but now that you bring it up . . .'

'Wait till I get my hands on him.'

'Look here, my dear husband.' For the first time that day she was tender. 'You don't have to pretend to me. If there is no money to buy the batteries, just say so. I'm willing to wait. Did you bring the salt?'

'I had no money.'

'Where did you put it?'

'Put what?'

'The money.'

'I didn't put it anywhere, I simply didn't have it, and that's that.'

'Yacobo,' she was tenderly sarcastic. 'Do you think we'll be able to afford salt for our food when your revolution succeeds?'

'Salt, that's all you can think about when I am talking about bigger and greater things.'

'Like what, for example?'

'Oh, like going into the army. Sergeant Yacobo! Yes sir.' He stood at attention and saluted. His eyes glared with a kind of murderous greed. 'Men! Spread out and search these houses, and don't leave a stone unturned. And if you find him, bring him to me. I'll deal with him personally.'

'Who? Who?' the wife asked beginning to get into the act.

'The Minister, stupid. Ah and here he comes. Now stand there and don't move. I know your salary and I know your background. Where did you get all that money from and in so short a time?'

'Ask him, Yacobo, ask him.'

'And how did you come by that beautiful wife of yours, uh? Now I'm going to give her to my men. Hi, hi, hi, hi. They haven't been near a female for months. She'll love it, her with her history. First you have a *coup* and then you declare a general election, what? Democracy, that's what I call it.'

He turned around to his wife and fixed her with those red blood-curdling eyes. He began to tremble with emotion.

'And now, it's the time of reckoning,' he spoke straight to her face. 'Mr Minister, is there anything you would like to say for yourself? Because my plan is to give you a fair trial and then hang you. I mean fair's fair, and there cannot be two ministers of the same position at the same time. I'm taking over. Do you hear me? I'm taking over from you stinking lot of thieves. You have lived on empty promises and the fat of the land.' He got hold of his wife by the neck. 'And now I'm going to make you spit it.'

'No, don't do it, Yacobo, don't do it,' she protested, half choked.

'Oh yes, I'm going to kill you, I'm going to kill you, you bastards. Look where I live, and look where you live. The hut and the castle. And what did you do to deserve those things? Nothing. Only a lot of lies about jobs and food, and the fight against disease and ignorance. And what jobs did we get? Tell me what job was I offered? Sanitary inspector, looking after the welfare of the shit-houses of the land. Now I'll tell you: that is where you should've been. Because that is where you belong. And right now that is were you are going. I'll drop you into the company of your friends the maggots, and there you'll find a stinking rest.'

'Yacobo, it's me, you're killing me. I'm not the minister.' Rozalia managed a stifled whisper.

'You are lying. And I'll kill you, thieving bastard.'

'No, no, don't, Yacobo. All I asked for was whether you had brought the salt or not. I don't even care where you've been all night. You have been fighting for the land. To move us to a better house. Yacobo, listen to me. It's me, your wife Rozalia.'

Yacobo squeezed her throat more and she began to sink to her knees. Then he released his grasp. She pulled back frightened, holding her neck. Yacobo screamed and went after her. She ran across the tiny room and tripped when her foot was caught in a hole in the mat. Yacobo pounced upon her. One hand held her down and the other pulled her clothes right up to her belly. He held them there and shifted his weight on to the hand that held the clothes. Then with his other hand he pulled off his trousers. He was breathing rapidly and foaming at the mouth. Rozalia acted by instinct. She parted her legs as if something within her told her that birth, violence and death were joined together in eternal communion. He was hot inside her; she convulsed and he felt her wrap him up and begin to suck the life out of him. When it came, it was like exploding into a vacuum. Great gushes of the incarnation. Live lava ascends the walls of the volcano to embrace the thunderbolt; it throbs, yielding milk and life and flowers and seeds. Their breathing was now slower and they lay there in silent communion. Yacobo looked at her, and she was his wife Rozalia. He had not felt like that with her for a long time. Maybe she still had a bit of life in her. She looked at him too and he appeared strong and healthy. He was still inside her.

'Yacobo.'

'Hmm?'

'You have been drinking.'

'Yes.'

'Did you bring the salt?'

'No.'

'Will you have your food without it.'

'I don't want any food.'

'I had also waited for you, but now I don't want any food either.'

They looked each other in the eyes, and moved on to their sides.

'Sorry, is my elbow hurting you?'

'No, but I'll buy you a nail-file for it tomorrow.'

They giggled. She snuggled up to him, and they fell asleep.

Across the open drainage, on the other side of the slum village, there was another man. His mud-wall dwelling was only a few yards away from the beer hall where drunks sat all night and ate watered dregs of Kwete beer; occasionally one of them would get up and go round the corner of the house. There he would pull up his dirty Kanzu, face the wall and, penis in hand, wait for the water to come.

There in a small house, smelling of drainage, urine and beer, Jeronimo sat. He was alone. Three or so hours ago he was a corporal, drinking brandy, dancing and enjoying himself. Two hours ago, he was a prophet, clad in banana leaves, and speaking words of wisdom and truth to a new-found disciple.

Now he sat alone in a tiny room, in a rat-infested, grass-thatched little dwelling. He thought to himself with disgust: Why all this pretension? Why all this play-acting? Maybe it is the desire to be things within one's vision yet beyond one's reach. The imagination takes you by the hand, and together you climb up the highest mountain. It invites you to look round. You look. And you see the great expanses of territory for human habitation. The fertile valleys, the vineyards, the castles. And you fly together and enter the castles and inhabit them. You are the host at the feast of great men. You propose the toast to a life of everlasting bliss. Everything is at your command. You clap your hands and the wine is brought to you. You clap again and the dancers begin. The prettiest women of the land are at your beck and call.

After imagination has shown you all this, the mountain on which you are standing collapses, and suddenly nobody is holding your hand. Then you discover that in fact these were wasted moments and that you have not moved an inch from the squalor in which you sat a while ago. Then what was it you were seeing a moment ago? A fantasy? Could it not come true and in fact are there not people who have made it come true? You realize that there are. But these are people who are the same as you and yet different; they are privileged. But why be made to see beyond your reach?

You begin to feel a prisoner of your birth, position and wealth. It is then that natural talent comes into play; you snatch these moments of unreality and turn them into temporary realities. But you always come back. And each time is more galling than the last. And therefore the compulsion to get away is stronger each successive time.

Jeronimo, alias the 'corporal', alias the 'prophet', had a clever and quick mind. But he was born to the wrong people. They had seen him through primary school and half of secondary school and they had run out of money. He had to stop his education and find work. It hurt him and hurt them too. For their will had been strong but their pockets weak.

'Why, why?' he shouted. No answer came from the four mud walls that surrounded him. A mouse ran from one hole on one side of the room, went across his lap and disappeared on the other side of the room. Jeronimo remained impassive as he sat like a Buddha thinking, talking silently to himself: Why above all, the incompatible combinations? Take Kigere, for example, he was a classmate of mine; and he always brought up the rear of the class. The tail-bearer we used to call him. And after high school it took him ten years to do a three-year law course. Look where he is now. And me, always first in the class. Look where I am!

He always looked at himself when he came back and was all by himself and alone with himself. There was nobody to act to. Nobody to play with. Yacobo, he always felt, was a bad influence on him. Perhaps if it had not been for him and his promises of easy escapism, Jeronimo might have been able to make something of himself. But now, like

Yacobo, he could not even keep his menial jobs. Yet somehow he felt it was impossible for him to break the hold of Yacobo on him. After one of those crazy excursions, Jeronimo had come and told himself, that was the last he would ever do. But every time a new occasion arose, he succumbed to the persuasions of the more hardened Yacobo, who was ten years his senior. In such an existence, evenings tended to be dull; and often Yacobo had turned up at Jeronimo's shack.

'Coming with us, Jeronimo?'

'No, I think, Yacobo, I think I'll take a day off.'

'Oh? And why? Abandoning your old friends, uh?'

'No, not exactly. I just feel a little tired.'

'He, he, he, she's quite a girl. You already feeling tired. Think I'll give her a try myself.'

Jeronimo didn't like that. He was the sentimental type. He would join Yacobo.

Sometimes it had been:

'Coming with us, Jeronimo?'

'No, Yacobo. I'm fed up with this whole thing and I'm pulling out.'

'Eh, what's this? Or are my ears deceiving me? Pulling out, did you say? And you think your old friends will let you off so you can spill the beans. They aren't that thick you know.' Unfortunately Jeronimo knew Yacobo only too well. So he would go. And so it went on. Jeronimo was telling himself: One of these days I'm going to put my foot down; and they'll have to kill me if they like, but I won't go. I wonder if they ever feel the same way as I do after these adventures?

A couple of mice ran up the wall and into the grass roof. They laughed wildly. A lizard, apparently scared, dropped, belly first on to the floor, and ran off at great speed. Jeronimo still stared ahead of him. In the distance he could hear crickets sing through their iron larynxes. No birds; the town was no place for them. Just bats and an occasional owl, which Jeronimo thought was a bird only by accident.

Suddenly he realized he was still wearing that ridiculous banana-leaf costume. He tore it off furiously and stood naked. He felt a kind of freedom but it did not last and the depression returned. He walked to the wall and placed his hands against it. Then in a series of sudden vigorous moves he banged his head against it. Lumps of dry mud tore off and fell at his feet. He picked them up and began to eat them. He liked the smell of dry mud.

Out in the cool night, four miles away, three bodies lay on the cold asphalt road. Machine-gun bullets had gone clean through them. The blood was beginning to clot and dry. In the morning one fly, and then others, would come and settle. Such was the end.

Of course when Jeronimo sat in his shack, eating dry mud off his wall, he did not know what had happened to the rest of the gang, though he half suspected it, having heard the burst of gun-fire some hours ago. He was making up his mind to get out. They had pulled out; their decision made for them by a man with a gun.

An owl perched on top of his house and began to cry. It was then that Jeronimo knew this was not just any other day; the worst was yet to come. The mice in the roof played housey and squealed. He took another bite at the mud and prepared for the morning.

6 The dew was already dry on the grass when the day started for Yacobo and Rozalia; they had had a late night, and the apple had again suckled the spider in the early part of the morning. When they were up, Rozalia cooked plantains swimming in groundnut sauce; Yacobo ate and was contented.

Then the sun burned the earth and a man had to get about. About five o'clock in the evening, Yacobo began to feel unsettled and wished to go visiting.

'Rozalia, I think I'll go and pay my respects to the Muluka chief, and do one or two other things,' he said to his wife.

'I suppose if you sat here for a whole day your manhood would drop off and you would become a woman. You must have sniffed at the feet of a dog when you were born; you can't stay in one place for as long as it takes to warm Mbooge leaves,' she said to him, though this time with tenderness.

'Only a jealous man sits around his wife all day. A good woman must be given space to breathe.'

'Skip the excuses and get on your way. I'll be waiting when you come back. Don't forget to bring the salt when you return.' Yacobo stopped and looked at her for a moment. Then he passed his hand through his hair to see what it looked like, sniffed under both his armpits and, without saying another word, went off to Jeronimo's house.

He did not live far away. At about five-thirty Yacobo arrived, but the door was shut and there was no sign of life.

'Jeronimo, Jeronimo, are you in there?' No reply. 'Jeronimo, are you in the house?'

'Who's there? Is that you, Yacobo? I don't want to see you.'

'Did I hear you right?'

'Yes, you did, I don't want to see you.'

'What kind of a welcome is that for a man who's been through all that trouble with you?'

'Yeah. Trouble is right. If it hadn't been for you, I wouldn't be shut up in this house as I am.'

'What happened? Some joker lock you in?'

'Stop shouting out there and letting the whole village know you eat locusts. I'm staying right where I am and I don't want to see you.'

'Come on, open the door for me and stop shifting the blame.'

'I can't open for you, I'm not dressed.'

'Get up then and get dressed. You aren't going to sleep all day.'

'I can't get dressed.'

'What's happened? You broke your arm or something?'

'I didn't break my arm or something. Anyway stop shouting out there. You sound as though you were weaned on the smoked meat of the Ngegeya bird.'

'Open the door or I'll break it.'

'Don't push too hard or you'll fall inside.' Yacobo pushed at the door gently and it opened. It was dark inside the house, so he lit a match and opened the window.

Jeronimo was folded up in one corner of the small room with bark cloth wrapped around him.

'Snap yourself together, man. Let's go and have some fun. What happened? You lost a relative or something?'

'Might have done better if I had lost a relative.'

'How do you mean?'

'I lost my shirt and trousers. You know they were the only clothes I had. It was your idea to turn their insides into an army uniform. Now I haven't anything to wear.'

Yacobo suppressed a chuckle as he remembered the prophet's scene the night before. 'Amen, Amen I say to you . . .' he broke out into loud laughter. 'I told you Jeronimo, you were a bit too clever for your own good. Now look what you've got yourself into. No clothes. And what'll happen if you are ordered out by the man you can't disobey? Your toilet is outside the house, isn't it?'

'Don't talk about it. You might make it happen.' He paused. 'Now, don't stand there staring at me, think of something. You got me into all this trouble: "Jeronimo, come let's go and have some fun, Jeronimo, let's go and have a kip, Jeronimo this, Jeronimo that." I'm sick and tired of your lot.'

'No need to get bitter. If the worst came to the worst, you could wear the bark cloth you have there. Only the army out there in the town would search you, for guns.'

'Guns! Now we've had it. I left that gun in the garden as well.'

'It doesn't matter. It hasn't got a name on it.'

'Name? No it hasn't.' Jeronimo sounded nervous.

'All right. Now we can't go out. What'll we do?' Yacobo asked.

'Well I don't know what you're going to do. As for myself, I'm just about to go to bed. I can't say I had a very good night last night,' Jeronimo replied.

'I told you, you should get married. Being alone, that's what it does to you. You get fed up with looking at yourself all the time.'

'I don't want to get married and it's about time you went back to your wife!'

'I can take care of my wife, thanks. Anyway she said she didn't mind.'

'And you believe her?'

'Why not? It suits me to.'

'All right, you're right. Now go because I'm finished with you.'

Yacobo felt this was getting serious. He approached Jeronimo, held him by the shoulders and shook him vigorously: 'Now listen to me, you blooming idiot. I save you from loneliness. I take you out for a good time. I've shown you this city and I've rubbed the greenness off your nose. And what do I get? Bloody ingratitude! All right, I'll leave you alone. I'll leave you alone in this house without clothes, and if your gun is found with your mousey finger-marks on it, I'll turn you in and collect that reward. And that'll teach you gratitude.'

Jeronimo tried to loosen Yacobi's grip. He looked into his eyes which were blood-shot and terrifying. He decided to play along.

'Let go, Yacobo. Let go, you're hurting me.' Yacobo loosened his grip. 'No need to take it that seriously, I was only joking.'

'Well, learn to think of better jokes.'

'All right, all right, keep your shirt on,' Jeronimo said, which brought his own nakedness back to mind.

The two men fell silent. Then after a while:

'Hey!' Yacobo said playfully. 'What shall we do then?'

'Well, anything really. I mean anything that doesn't demand that I should be properly dressed.'

'Well, all right, that's better. Let's play a game.'

'Which game?'

'The horse and the jockey-back.'

'No I don't want that one.'

'Why?'

'I just don't want it, that's all.'

'Got a better idea?'

'Let's play cards.'

'No, I hate cards.'

'All right, so we skip the games,' Jeronimo thought he was putting the seal on to the matter.

'No, we're going to play jockey-back whether you like it or not.'

'Well I don't like it.'

'Now we begin,' commanded Yacobo. 'I'm the horse. You're the jockey.'

'All right,' Jeronimo agreed.

'Now what kind of a horse am I? A political horse, an ecclesiastical hobby horse or what?'

'I don't know. Whatever you like.'

'Now come on, it takes two to play, what kind of a horse am I?' Yacobo demanded.

'A political horse.'

'Right, I'm a political horse. I'm the masses and you're the politician.'

'That's right.' Jeronimo was beginning to warm up. 'But I'm not dressed,' he protested.

'And since when have you been dressed? Anyway, remember I'm the masses and I'm not supposed to see you're naked.'

'Right.'

Yacobo grinned and went down on all fours.

'Sit on my back, come on, sit on my back.' He was getting excited. 'Sit on my back, Jeronimo.'

Jeronimo, stark naked, mounted Yacobo's back and cracked the whip with his lips: 'Giddyup, jackass, giddy-giddygiddy.'

'Ouououweeeec,' Yacobo gave a horsey cry.

'Giddyup, giddyup.'

'You're riding me hard now; more, more, drive me harder. I'm the masses.'

'Now look ahead of you. Hey! Faster! You see the green pastures over yonder? That's where you really want to go. Because that's where I'm going. Now I'm riding you. I ride on your back to the pastures of my dreams. Now do you feel it?'

'Yes I feel it. Ride me faster.'

'You like it, don't you. You like to carry me on your back. You need my weight on your back, don't you, you horsey mass?'

'I do, master, I do. And when we reach the green pastures beyond, what will you give me?'

'A blade of grass, jackass and then another. I mustn't give you too much because you'll grow too fat, and that's no good for your speed. Besides I need the rest of the grass myself, to stuff my ideologies with. Giddyup, jackass.'

'Ouououowweeeee.'

'And do you see the moon?'

'Yes, master I see it.'

'And the sun and the stars?'

'Yes, master, I see them.'

'I'll climb to the pedestal and I'll give you their shadows.'

'Ride me, master, ride me hard. I'll take the blade of grass and I'll take the shadows. And when you dig the spurs hard into my flesh I'll rise to new heights of excitement. But when you are done and finished with me, master, what will you do with me?'

'I'll think of that, jackass. Giddyup.'

They rose to new heights of fantasy. Yacobo was foaming at the mouth, Jeronimo was riding as hard as he could, springing up and down on Yacobo's back.

'And when you finish with me, what'll you do to me?'

'A good horse is a running horse, jackass. When you outlive your usefulness I'll shoot you and kill you, jackass.'

Yacobo stopped suddenly and sprang to his feet. He threw Jeronimo against the mud wall. Jeronimo screamed and held his head in agony.

'What did you say, you naked sinner, what did you say?' Yacobo demanded.

'But you asked me, Yacobo, you asked me.'

'Repeat it and I'll send your spirit to your unlamented ancestors,' Yacobo approached Jeronimo in a threatening manner. 'Repeat it: you ride me and then you kill me – go on.'

'B-b-b-b-but it was only a game. Only a game, Yacobo.'

Yacobo breathed a deep long-drawn breath. He was calming down. 'Yeah it was only a game,' he conceded.

The two men fell silent again. Jeronimo massaged his head where it had hit the wall. After some time he broke a piece of mud off the wall and began to chew it. He turned to Yacobo. 'Would you like some dry mud?' he offered Yacobo a piece.

'No, Jeronimo, I'm trying to give it up. Thanks all the same.'

Jeronimo ate alone.

A short while elapsed and then Yacobo spoke. 'Look, get dressed in that bark cloth and come home with me. We'll eat that fat chicken together.'

'All right,' Jeronimo agreed quietly.

He wrapped himself in the bark cloth and they went off.

'Is that you, Yacobo?' Rozalia shouted out from the house as they arrived just before dark.

'Yes, it's me and a friend, Jeronimo.'

She came out to greet them.

'Eh, what happened to the gentleman's clothes?' she asked.

'He lost them,' Yacobo answered.

'Lost them? How?'

'You see we were playing a game. We took off our working clothes and hung them up on the fence and when we looked away some thief must have taken them,' Yacobo said.

'Oh dear. What kind of game was that?'

'Tennis. Is dinner ready?'

'Yes, did you bring the salt?'

Yacobo looked at Jeronimo as if blaming him for not having brought the salt. But Jeronimo knew nothing of the matter, yet he pleaded: 'It's not my fault, honest!'

'Well you'll have to eat the food without the salt,' she said.

'I still say it's a waste,' said Jeronimo as he ate another mouthful, 'I mean such a fat chicken and no salt. Why, the gravy tastes like a cow's urine.'

'I see Rozalia is getting some help from you,' Yacobo retorted.

'How do you mean?'

'He won't understand,' Rozalia said to Jeronimo. 'He won't understand. You needn't waste your saliva telling him. How many times have I asked him to bring me salt on his way home. But every time he forgets.'

'Forgets what? To buy a pound of salt?'

'No, to get the money to buy the salt,' said Yacobo, hoping for a laugh.

Suddenly Jeronimo jumped up. He threw away the morsel of food he was just about to eat, repeatedly slapped his cheeks and buttocks.

'What's wrong, Jeronimo? Have you swallowed a bone or something?' Yacobo asked, putting down a chicken bone he had been eating loudly.

'The tickets,' said Jeronimo.

'What tickets? What about them?'

'I left my poll tax tickets in my clothes. They've got my name and everything on them. That's even worse than finger-prints.'

'You fool, you damned idiot.' Yacobo was getting mad.

'I'm not sure I understand,' intervened Rozalia. 'Surely if a thief takes your clothes, he's got his finger-prints to worry about, not yours.'

'Eh, er, what's that?'

'I said that if . . .'

'Yeah we heard,' Yacobo said. 'We'll explain later. We must go and get those clothes back, Jeronimo.'

'Well, we can't do it now. It's well past curfew hours.'

'If they get them before we do, you'll be in curfew for life. Those are your poll tax tickets in there, not mine.'

'What do you mean? We were in it together.'

'In what, you two?' She was getting suspicious.

'In the game of tennis. If he doesn't get his tickets back he would be arrested by the tax collectors any time he went to town.'

'He isn't going to town anyway. He hasn't any clothes. I mean the police would have him in before the tax collectors ever set eyes on him.'

'Shut up, woman, we're trying to think.'

'That's a change. You must lose poll tax tickets more often. It helps you exercise your brain.'

'I told you I was wrong to marry her. She's getting too clever these days. That's bad in a woman.'

'Well it seems to be bad in a man too, since so many of you are avoiding it,' Rozalia replied.

'Shut up, woman, or I'll feed your ears to my dog.'

'You have no dog . . .'

'Christ almighty! The Lord sent Moses the rainbow sign, no more water, the woman next time!' Yacobo said, getting up and raising his arms to the roof. 'What do we do, Jeronimo, what do we do?'

'We must get them back before they find them.'

'I thought you two said they were stolen.'

'Hold my hands, Jeronimo, hold my hands before I kill

her,' Yacobo was scratching his head and pacing about the room.

'Mind how you scratch your head,' said Rozalia. 'Some of us are still eating and we want our food clean.'

'Poor clean food, pushed into your dirty inside. Jeronimo, shut her up for me. She's confusing me.'

'Shut up, woman.'

'Not you too!'

There was a moment of silence. Then Jeronimo said in a depressed perplexed voice: 'It is hard to say it, but we must wait till the morning.'

Yacobo found this difficult to accept. But after some reflection he sighed and said: 'I suppose you're right. Those army men will shoot at anything that moves after curfew hours.' He paused, and then added, 'You can stay here for tonight.'

Jeronimo agreed. Rozalia looked at the two men, wondering. She shrugged her shoulders and resumed eating.

7   In a minute, Joe and Simon would be back on the long road. They had taken bark cloths from the bedroom and covered their bodies. Then Joe had gone and told Anzera the sad news. She wailed and tore at her breast. She would keep mother company until the relatives arrived.

They took two bananas each, and said good-bye to Joe's mother. She didn't answer; she only looked at them and shook her head up and down three times. Joe stood for a moment and let his arms drop to his thighs, almost in resignation. But the determination returned. He looked at his mother again, swallowed bitterly, turned away and began to walk. Simon said: 'We'll be back,' and turned to follow Joe.

There weren't many cars around at that time in that part of the country and it was many hours before Joe and Simon heard the noise of one approaching.

'Step on your big toe, Simon. We must get a lift. I'm tired.' Then the car appeared around the corner. They waved and it stopped. It was an old and ramshackle car and creaked wherever there were pieces of metal left. Elsewhere, fibres and strings had replaced the metal.

The driver was kind and did not ask many questions. Joe and Simon looked haggard, but there was a shine beneath the dirt that showed they were not dangerous. He let them in and they hoped nothing would go wrong with the car. As they passed the house of Zimenya, Joe thought of the fig tree, the bark cloth and his mother. He must get back before the funerals.

Soon they reached the place in the road where the soldiers had been filling in the trench. Darkness had begun to restrict their view. The driver didn't fall into the hole though. He knew it well. As he approached it he saw two trucks parked by the road. They were army trucks. He gave quick instructions to Joe and Simon. The soldiers must be waiting in the grass by the roadside. His passengers were not to say anything unless closely questioned.

At the trench they stopped. Nothing moved. The driver got out of the car to examine the trench. It had only been partly filled. He was puzzled; his car would never be able to drive into and then out of it. And whatever had happened to the soldiers in the trucks? They must be around in the tense silent air. The grass showed nothing but he knew they were in there. What was he going to do? He was afraid and began to feel the guns pointing at him. Taking hold of himself he pulled a torch out of his pocket and flashed it at the bushes along the roadside, on the pretext that he was looking for some firm ground for his car to circumvent the trench.

He held his breath and stood in amazed silence. A heap of bodies lay piled, one on the other. He had in fact dug the trench; but he did not think at the time that his catch would be half as satisfying. He got back into the car. He did not tell his passengers, only drove round the ditch and continued their journey.

As the night grew darker they decided to stop and wait for the morning. They turned off the road and made the car their house for the night.

At first light the chill of the morning blew through the car windows and caught the ears of the driver. He woke up and tried to shake the others awake; they were deeply asleep, since they had not slept for a long time. After some effort they managed to shake their heads clear. The car was given a push to start it, and they resumed the journey towards the city, Joe and Simon nodding off to sleep as they went.

After many hours of driving, the city appeared on the hills in the distance. The number of soldiers they passed progressively increased. Then they were upon the cyclists going to work, and more and more cars. Joe and Simon and the driver had not discussed the motives for their journeys. And when the excitement grew in them as the city approached, they still did not tell each other.

Now they were at the outskirts of the city. The air was electric and one felt drastic things had taken place during the night. Soon, for Joe and Simon, the real search would start; they had to find their men. They did not realize that their travelling companion had set himself a similar aim. At times like this people tend to work in isolated groups. It is a sign of the break-down in confidence between the people.

They reached the main approach to the city and turned a corner. And there it was, a road block. They had seen many of these in their lifetime, but they had never meant so much to them. Road blocks had been things they passed on their way to the office or the butcher's shop. Now the road block was the symbol of what they were fighting, the symbol of what they had to defeat. Many times before they had passed it as a matter of routine and no real fear gripped them. Now they were afraid, but determined.

They went up to it cautiously. They were there; soldiers in front of them, behind them, soldiers everywhere. They stood with drawn bayonets or lay and took aim at things that moved; they would probably shoot at them give or take a bit of luck.

A soldier waved for them to stop, and they did. 'Come out of there.'

They got out of the car without protest. To Joe this was strange. He had protested before when he was less angry than he was now. But he realized that when you have nothing more concrete in view than a pair of principles, you tend to verbalize your protest even where you know it will not change anything. Now he had a specific fighting tactic in view; to find the men. He was keen to stay alive until he had done so. But as he looked at the crowd at the barrier he wondered. It was the way they passed the soldiers, their demeanour looked to him more like a posture of acceptance than planned, temporary, acquiescence. Joe waited for his turn.

'Now stand there, you three,' a soldier commanded and they did. A timid frightened man was brought and planted in front of them.

'Now is it one of these?' a soldier asked the man.

He scrutinized them, his eyes moving from one to the other and then back again. His eyes stopped. 'It's him, sir, that's right. It's him.' He was pointing at Simon. Simon was confused and startled. He resisted a defensive laugh which such feelings always tend to provoke if one is not on one's guard. The silly fellow must be making some mistake.

'Come with us, the others you may go.'

'What? Where are you taking him. This is Simon my serv ... I mean my friend. He has been with me for the past two days and he has done nothing.'

The soldiers just gave him one look and brushed him aside.

'Listen, you're making a terrible mistake, you're getting the wrong man,' Joe pleaded.

'Wrong man for what?' a soldier asked.

'How should I know. I don't even know why you're arresting him.'

'Then how do you know he is the wrong man?'

'Er, because he has been with me all this time, and . . .'

'Is that so? Maybe you ought to come with us too.'

'All right . . . I will . . .'

'No, Joe,' Simon intervened. 'You carry on with the work. I haven't done anything wrong. They'll find that out sooner or later; and I'll rejoin you when I am released.'

Joe could not believe what he was seeing. Will there be no end to this? What wrong could Simon possibly have committed? He had not let him out of sight. Or had he? He turned to the crowd that wanted to pass the road block on their way to work in the city. Then he turned to the soldiers and back to the crowd again. He wanted to accuse the soldiers. Impeach them, appeal to the conscience of the people. Incite rebellion. But the crowd just stared right back at him, eyes clearly disapproving: leave us alone, all we want is to get through here as soon as possible. We must not be late for our work in the city. Our pay will be cut. And who would want to employ trouble-makers? Joe could hear the thoughts beyond the eyes of individuals: I have children, and they are at school. I must look after them, and I'm not going to do it by losing my job; certainly not trying to save a man I've never seen before. Don't look at me; I didn't start all this. I mean I was dropped into this country and found it exactly as it is; and my duty is to get through it alive. Well I mean I'll die sometime, but I must get through life alive . . . preserve myself, natural instinct really; you can't blame me, you know; all right to go ahead and blame me; and what good will it do you? I mean we have to survive, don't we?

Joe felt sickened by those cowardly, timid, impotent looks. He felt like yelling: All right, go on and preserve yourselves, you putrefying masses of human refuse devoid of all honour. You think you're alive. But I've got news for you. You're dead. As dead as those soldiers you see in front of you. You've passed from life and descended into limbo. And there your bodies float in the unrevenged blood of your brethren whose courage was too much for the rulers of this land.

He looked and Simon was being led away. Something gave way in his stomach. The feeling was too much for him and he sat down.

'Get out of the way, these people want to pass. They've work to go to. Clean-living people, in clean clothes. Not like you. Now get up before I arrest you.'

Joe got up and moved.

A little way on, Simon was brought in front of an irate officer.

'Now where did you buy it from?'

'Buy the what?'

'Now don't start playing games with me; I'm no child. Where, I repeat, did you get it from?'

'I don't know what you're talking about.'

'Sir!'

'Sir.'

'Tell us then where you got it from.'

'The what?' Simon was driven to the limit.

'The poison that killed the soldiers.'

'Which soldiers?'

'Oh? How many types of soldiers do you know of? The resistance?'

'I know nothing of the kind.'

'Then tell us where you got that poison that killed the soldiers.'

The driver of the ramshackle car had managed to stay within earshot. He was jumping to the wrong conclusion. All those bodies he saw. He felt like hugging Simon, but he thought better of it.

'Did you hear me? Sergeant, explain.'

The soldier slapped Simon in the face. The blood went into Simon's mouth, but he did not spit.

'Now are you going to talk or shall I send you to head-quarters? They make dead men speak there.'

'I told you I know nothing of the poison or the soldiers.'

The officer paused and slapped his cane repeatedly in the palm of his left hand. He then turned and walked around in a small circle and returned to face Simon. 'Now let's take it from the beginning. The soldiers went to the butcher's shop near Mvule Hill. They wanted to requisition some meat. They looked for the butcher but they couldn't find him anywhere. ('Lie' Simon thought to himself.) So they just took the meat. Now as it turned out the meat was poisoned. And I'm sure it was before it was taken out of the shop. So you are responsible for the death of at least twenty soldiers.'

Simon wished for a moment he had really been responsible. Then he said: 'I told you, sir, I know nothing about this. And this is the first time I have heard of it.'

'Really? Then do you deny that you were seen at

the butcher's shop with a lot of his other friends that morning?'

'No, I don't deny that. But then I left for the country and have not been around town since.'

'You're not a good liar. What part of the country have you been to?'

'Masajja.'

'Is that right?'

'Yes.'

'Then you must know of the two lorries of soldiers massacred there at a trench across the road.'

'A what? At a trench?'

'See? You're lying. You haven't been to Masajja.'

'Sergeant, take him to headquarters.' Then he turned to Simon; 'I have a feeling somehow you aren't going to like this.' Simon was led away. He didn't see Joe as he went.

8 Sometimes, Joe thought, sanity merely declares a betrayal of values, the concrete symptom of the dishonesty to one's experience. It is a sign that the victim has escaped, deserted and is hiding away somewhere beneath the surfaces.

There he stood, with this cretinous crowd around him, he had witnessed an arrest which might lead to Simon's death, and it was beyond his powers to intervene. Barely three nights ago he had been raided, driven out of his house and deprived of his possessions. At his family home, he had found five massacred nieces and cousins, and a raped mother staring at their mutilated bodies. He had spent two days and two nights on the roads, his skin itched and burned, and his knee had a consuming pain. And he, Joe, just stood there in full possession of his mental faculties; moved, angry, tired, dejected, bloody fed-up, but stark raving sane. What right had he to feel sane? Any person in their proper senses would have gone mad ages ago. But what does a man do against the evil powers of the world? Fight? This way he is drawn into using the same means against which his soul is campaigning. He is pulled down to the level of the beasts who have made his blood boil in the first place. Evil drives out the good until the devil inhabits every corner of the world. What can one do? That, unfortunately seldom even reduces the number of bad men; and it probably means one less good one. Besides, writing has a way of placating the need that inspires it. It gives the splendid feeling that the writer has done his duty, and that if humanity will not heed his message, so much the worse for humanity. However, the point about problems is not doing one's bit, but getting them solved. That often means a sacrifice few of us are willing to make, though we know very well that one day we shall just lie on our beds and die for no good reason other than that our time has come.

As he stood in the midst of the soldiers and the crowd that was trying to pass them Joe's head towered above the rest. There was a heaviness about his body; drops of sweat trickled down his back and itched like lice crawling all over him. His face was wet and the area around his jutting chin felt stiff with the bristles which had grown during two days without Phillips Rotary Action. He searched his pockets for a handkerchief, but he hadn't got one. He scratched behind his ears, producing a shiver down his back, and then rubbed the sweat off his face with the palm of his hand.

'Well he's gone. I think we'd better continue our journey.' The voice was that of the driver who had brought them all the way back to the city, the road block and the arrest. He could not hold it against the driver. But if he had not picked them up, maybe when Joe's and Simon's anger subsided after a long walk, they would have changed their minds about getting back to the city and returned to the house and sat with mother to stare at, and then bury, the mutilated bodies of his relations. Not that that was any good either; sitting there and staring at the dead while their murderers go free, scaring food out of the hands of frightened people.

'I said, maybe we better continue . . .'

'I heard you,' Joe cut in, then he remembered his manners. 'You'll excuse me if I'm a little abrupt but I've had rather a hard time these last few days.'

'You've the marks of it on your face. Maybe you ought to come with me to my house. I'll see to it that you are taken care of until you're in a better condition to go wherever it is you are going.'

'No, no, no, I appreciate your kindness, but I couldn't impose . . .' He stopped. Imposing himself? He remembered the hospitality he and Simon were given at that house in the country when all they had done was just stopped to ask the way. The happy faces of the man and his wife, when Joe and Simon had dug into the food like two wild beasts on the run came to mind. There was the food and then the love that came with it. Zimenza was happy because Joe and Simon had eaten. It was not a Christian offering of food to God disguised in the persons of two itinerant men; it was an offer of food to two hungry men. When you have eaten you do not raise your eyes past your hosts towards the distant heavens and thank them for your pounded yam or whatever food you happen to have in your mouth. You look straight at the hosts and thank them. Giving is a pleasure. The pleasure comes directly from the act, but mealy-mouthed Christian modern charity has turned giving into a sacrifice from which, by some masochistic trick, the individual is supposed to get satisfaction. He does this by lifting up his eyes and his soul and imagining that he is giving not the miserable creature in front of him, but to the eternal God above. Such arrogance! Men do not deal with men any more. They deal with God and thereby with men. At any rate that's what they think they are doing. Humanity has cheated itself of its claim to its own status. People fail to see the man in front of them as a man worthy of charity and all the other virtues in their own right. They look beyond him and his misery to the elusive presences in the distance. They are charitable, not so that the being to whom charity is directed may be rid of his suffering, but so that one's place in heaven may be made that little bit more certain. Fallen humanity no longer matters, just the feather-bedding of one's heavenly nest. This self-directed charity has become a self-inflicted evil, and we all play up to it: 'No thank you very much, I wouldn't like to inconvenience you ... Oh, thank you very much but you should not have done it ...' To crown it all, when you are given something and are happy to say 'Thank you' the reply comes with the dead weight of a stone: 'Don't mention it!'

'Shit, man, where is your home, I'm coming,' Joe heard himself articulate the line.

'I beg your pardon?'

'Didn't you invite me just now to your home?'

'Yes I did, but that hardly calls for the shit.'

'Forget it. I'll come anyway. Slip of the tongue. You know, er ...?'

'Moses, that's my name, Moses.'

'You know, Moses, bit by bit we're all being dehumanized whether we like it or not. We're all being pushed through a great, revolving machine, and we come out the other end as simple, turgid sausages wrapped in a piece of skin.'

'Don't I know it, man, don't I know it.' Moses was a young engineer who had studied in America. He had a dark brown complexion and well sculptured though sizeable features. It was not so much the shape of each individual part of the face which made him look attractive; it was rather the combination of the several dark features which gave the kind of esoteric beauty of a modern piece of sculpture. He was nearing thirty-five now and at five feet six inches he was quite big for his size; a statistic not lost on the local girls.

After the United States he had returned to his country with great ideas about development, and a desire to show some of those damned, insulting Yankees that Africans could really pull it off. So, on getting home he joined one of the post-graduate courses at his own home university to do a bit of rounding off. It was then that the rot had set in. What a crowd of college students! They had all the intellectual warmth of an iceberg, and the committed involvement of a computer. A bunch of intellectual mercenaries, assembly line civil servants, that's what the college was turning out. Oh, highly intelligent, the cream of the young men at high school; but now sealed and waiting to be delivered to their respective pigeon holes. You could see it in their faces. They could not wait to graduate and get into these Government hire-purchase cars and low rental housing. They fancied a title on which to pin their names, like 'Tsetse Fly Area Research Programmer'; which did not even mean anything as sensible as a birth control unit for the creatures.

When the first troubles had overtaken his country, he had tried to organize opposition to go to the central power among the intellectuals, but with no luck. So he decided to go it alone whenever he could. The trench had been his most recent exploit and by digging it he was really doing his duty.

The old car jaunted along, with Moses at the wheel, and Joe apprehensively by his side.

'Nice old machine you have here; a bit on the aged side, but I should say you still have a few thousand miles left in her.'

'Oh, I only use this one for special occasions,' Moses replied.

'Really? Do you go to work then in a vintage model?'

'Gha, you are funny.'

'Oh I hadn't realized,' Joe paused. 'I say, did you really take a good look at that soldier at the barrier? Evil, cruel, but frightened. In fact it is the other way round. Frightened, therefore evil and cruel. You would be surprised on how many levels of social consciousness different people in the same society can live at the same time. I should say a lot of those fellows still have the psychological self-protectiveness required in the state of nature.'

'Come again?'

'I said that some of these fellows still live in the Hobbesian natural state, as far as their psychological reaction to social environment is concerned. You know what I mean? No. Actually I have never believed in the American educational system when it comes to specialization.'

The car lurched into a deep rut, and Joe knocked his head on the windscreen. He held his face in his palm. 'They don't make windscreens like that any more,' he said. 'They just provide you with a good suspension system. I say, is it very far to where you live?'

Moses did not reply. His attention seemed fixed to some object far beyond the confines of the fashionable neighbourhood in which they were now driving. A few lamp posts down the road and they pulled into an approach which led to a beautiful house situated in the middle of well-kept gardens. The house was on a slope and gave the impression of hugging the hill. Coming in from the front you could enter at ground floor level, and coming from the back, you entered the basement. There were rocks around which the constructors had not bothered to remove but which had been turned to good decorative use, so that the house seemed to grow out of the hill. This **was** Moses's house. His gleaming Mercedes Benz 220 **SE** crouched in the garage like a sphynx among the pyramids. Moses stopped the car and got out to open the door of the house. But he halted as if remembering again that he had someone with him. He smiled, slightly embarrassed, and invited Joe to come in. Moses had superb taste. Red patterned carpet, gold curtains and a low level suite of chairs in a shade of dark yellow. On the walls a Jimo Akolo, in his early, rustic period with shades of green, yellow and white; a violent Ignatius Sserulyo in purples, gold and red; and some other painters who were obviously of the newer generation as Joe could not rapidly recognize them. In recesses in the wall and on stands in the spaces, were a valuable collection of antiques. Moses asked Joe to sit down. But Joe was staring at an Ife piece of the sculpture and his mind was full of ideas.

'Oh, that's an unusual piece I picked up recently in Lagos. Quite difficult to get out of the country. But nothing is impossible between two lovers of art. I loved the sculpture, and the gentleman at the customs simply adored the watermark on a five-pound note. Great connoisseur I was given to understand. I have his particulars should you ever wish to make a collection,' Moses explained.

'I have a modest collection of my own, but nothing as magnificent as this. Do you really approve of bribery?'

'Of course I don't, but then I don't approve of sex outside marriage either – for my sisters.' Moses laughed.

There was something suspicious. There had to be. What was a man of this stature doing in an old car, wearing

tattered clothes, far out in the country at a time like this?
He had money, education, an impeccable and expensive
taste; he was unmarried, had relaxed scruples, and a disguise. Joe leapt to the conclusion he must be a spy. Probably
he was in the pay of some foreign power or the government; and Joe had no intention of getting on the wrong
side of either of them. He had first to cultivate this young
man.

'I must say this is a place I should like to live in. But
then I should probably not be able to afford it,' Joe
said.

'Nonsense, of course you could. If you were an engineer
like myself. I supervised the construction of the house.
A friend drew up the plans for peanuts, and . . . would you
care for a brandy?'

'Yes, thank you very much.'

'I have some very fine brandy here. A friend at one of
the embassies in town gets it for me. Otherwise I wouldn't
be able to afford it. I met him in America years ago as a
student. And the last time I went to one of those official
parties who should crop up but old Akim – Commercial
attaché . . . Say when.'

'That's fine, thank you. What do you think is going to
happen?'

'Happen to what?'

'To the country. Do you think the change is permanent?'

'No changes are permanent. The government of this
country seems to abide by the law of eternal change. Everyone is in it for what he can get out of it. That's the trouble.'

There was a pause before Joe asked in a worried voice:

'What do you think is going to happen to Simon; my friend at the barrier?'

'Oh, I don't know. They'll probably shoot him to bits. Poor devil. Have you two been doing anything I should know about?'

There was a chilly feeling in Joe's spine and it stiffened. He is a spy. Don't let a thing out. Anyway you have done nothing so far. This man is a corrupt spy. He bribes Nigerian customs officials, and then lies to me about his house. Joe had to find out.

'Poor devil,' Joe said. 'I suppose I have to put him out of my mind for the time being. You were telling me about the house. I still should say that putting it up, even under your supervision, must have cost you a pretty penny.'

'Well, let's say it would have.'

'How do you mean?'

'I mean they all do it, you know.'

'They all do what? No, I don't know.'

'Oh, come on, you ain't that green, baby. Nobody can prove it, see? A few noughts here in the estimate, a little bulldozer overtime there and the bricks begin to pour in; the motor begins to roll and a man can dig himself a pretty hole like this one. No bother. Just a plain understanding with the truck drivers; underpaid brutes, they really do welcome an extra penny. You get your own bricklayers, and so who is hurt?'

Moses paused and looked at Joe who was gripped in silent amazement. So how could he place Moses? Corrupt, yes, and corrupting. How did he ever get himself pushed together with this man; and at a time when he was so set on fighting against these things?

'Hey, come on now. Did I say something wrong? You look so all . . .'

'Say something wrong? You people talk as though it is an achievement to be able to pull off those dirty tricks.'

'Well, isn't it?' Moses said with a wide gesture of his arm, sweeping the whole room into view.

'Achievement, indeed; and you are really very proud of it. You really are proud of it! Now how do you expect everybody else to be fair and just when you . . .?'

'Did I say anything about being fair and just? The driver gets his cut and so does the bulldozer man. I pay the bricklayer and I supervise the construction.'

'And the taxpayer pays for the bricks, uh? And that's fair, Moses?'

'You got it all wrong, Joe. He doesn't pay for the bricks because I take 'em; he pays for the bricks because somebody is sure going to take 'em. Right? So I don't take the bricks, and the Minister will probably take twice as many.'

'And what makes you so sure that if you take them he won't take his lot anyway?'

'Well then if he does, we can nick him for the whole lot when the inquiry comes after the *coup d'état*. Right, Joe? These bastards deserve whatever is coming to them.'

'And you think you are going to get away with it; you think . . .?'

'Get away with what, Joe?' Moses was getting agitated.

'Get away with theft, get away with . . .?'

'Damn it, man,' Moses hit the table with the glass of brandy in his hand. It broke and scattered bits of glass and liquid all around the room. 'Damn it, damn it.' There was the silence that precedes an explosion.

138

But Joe was not letting up. He had always wanted to confront one of these thieving servants of the Government and really knock him.

'And what makes you think you can get away with it, I said?'

'Joe, look at me, look me straight in the face. Do you think I'm a thief?'

'Well appearances have a way . . .'

'Shit, man, screw your appearances. I'm tired of you moralizing lot. Tell me, Joe, there've been, let me see how many *coups d'état* since you came back here with your highfalutin ideas about African Socialism, African Democracy and African you-name-it we've-got it? Eh, how many *coups d'état*? And what've you done about it? Now come on, Joe, tell me.'

'You're not going to shift the argument from yourself, Moses; those tricks don't work with me. All I want to know is . . .'

'What tricks don't work with you? Too damn clever, yes? Oh I've read your screaming stuff in the papers, and I wonder whatever made you stop writing. It was a nice way to escape. The gallantry of the pen, Joe? Come on, let me see you pull out your pen and scare the hell out of me.' He paused to catch his breath. 'It's comfort you're after, Joe, like everybody else, and you're not fooling me. You can't fight a revolution from an emerald green velvet sofa?'

He must be a spy, thought Joe. How did he know I had an emerald green velvet sofa. He's only trying to get me to spy all he knows about the revolutionaries. But I know nothing about them so I'm safe. Let's press on with the argument.

'African Socialist?' Moses continued. 'Honestly, in your comfort and those businesses? Some of you African Socialists make Adam Smith look flaming red by comparison.'

'Now it's no use you trying to pull out my earlier ideas and using them against me in order to escape the reality of my argument. I'm talking about the house, the bricks and the bulldozer. I'm talking about the taxpayer's money.'

'I'm a taxpayer too and don't forget it. And I believe in getting back what I pay in. I wish to God there were more taxpayers like me, so the politicians wouldn't have so much to waste on themselves.'

'Then why pay the taxes in the first place? Keep them and save yourself the bother of getting them back by your devious means. Anyway you seem to have got a darn sight more in return than you paid in.'

'Don't most people in society do or wish to do that? Get more out of it than they ever put in?'

'And that doesn't mean they are right either. And what's more, there may be legitimate ways of doing it.'

'Like what for example? Upping the prices a little at your string of shops, Joe? Contrive scarcity? Defend legal cases which you know you are bound to lose? Run off to the countryside whenever there is a *coup d'état*? We know about you, Joe. Clever Joe. Cynical Joe. Escapist extraordinaire. Trouble with you, Joe, is you haven't got a mirror. You are so busy looking at everybody else you don't see them look at you; and therefore you don't see yourself.'

'That may be so. But I know a house built on taxpayer's

money when I see one. And that's what I'm talking about. Corruption.'

'Boy, you seem to think corruption only means adding a figure here and cutting one there. What about the corruption of the spirit? What about the withdrawal from reality and retreat into false intellectualism? What about your kind of corruption? It's easier. All you need is a good pen and a fine sense of humour and you can scribble the revolutionary spirit out of your system. It's respectable and it pays well. Right, Joe?'

'At least it's more honest.'

'More honest than what? Boy, you really get me. Joe, it's no use trying to get away from it, you have established your reputation. In the last analysis all you're interested in is Joe, and that's a fact.'

The two men were now standing, with Moses pacing up and down the room. Joe was almost immobile. He had not washed for days and his knee ached. Perhaps he should not have let himself in for an argument like that. Not the way he was feeling anyway. But on the other hand how could he have let such a display of social irresponsibility go without comment? He would never have been able to face himself after that. Well, all right, he would have been able to face himself, but it would have been painful.

He looked at the glass in his hand and discovered it still held some brandy, he swallowed it in one gulp. His face contorted and his nostrils widened a little.

Across the room to the left, Moses stood staring out of the window into the garden. In his mood of excitement and anger he could not have noticed the roses and the bougainvilia. White and coloured butterflies fluttered about, tossed by the wind. One bee, and then another collected yellow pollen on their legs and left in the direction of their hives. Soon the honey would flow and men would go and take it, and eat it as a matter of human right. The flowers stretched their petals and let the bees bother themselves with the pollen in almost derisive detachment like a prostitute. Why don't people go to the flowers and collect the pollen themselves, or better still make the bloody pollen itself. At the same time, however, these things had nothing to do with Moses who stood staring out of the window. Then in a sudden movement Moses turned from the window and faced Joe. For a worried moment Joe did not know what was going to happen to him. He fixed Joe with his eyes and said: 'All right, Joe, let's get down to brass tacks. If you're so full of social responsibility what are you going to do about *this coup d'état*? Or have you done something already? I've looked at you ever since I picked you up, but I was too unbelieving to ask any questions. This isn't like you at all, Joe. Come on, let's hear it.'

'I don't know if I haven't done my share of suffering already.'

'Who talked about suffering? I'm talking about solutions. What are we to do to solve this endemic political mess?'

'Solve it? You mean you want me to help you overthrow the politicians so you can become one yourself and steal twice as many bricks from the government supplies?'

'Cut the nonsense, Joe. Maybe I shouldn't have told you about my house. You've told me nothing about yourself. But I've known the price tags in your shops and your *coup d'état* drill, as you call it among your friends. And I say that when it comes to social irresponsibility, dishonesty to causes, feathering one's nest, you are every bit as guilty as the next man. Only you have done better out of it than most; and you have the audacity to stand there and accuse me of feeding on the fat of the nation.'

'Well, aren't you?'

'I'll admit I am. And that's more than you can do for yourself. That's why no good will ever come of you because you never admit it when you're in the wrong. Now tell me what you have been doing out there in the country? And who was that man with you?'

Joe said to himself: This man is a spy. He has a nice line of questioning. Don't let him take you in. Anyway what can you tell him? The facts about the soldiers? He doesn't want to know. What he is after is what you have done. And that is naught. Probably if you told him your mother had been raped he would break out and laugh. 'I've done nothing. I was going to the country and the soldiers took my car. Simon is my servant, or at least was before he became my brother and they took him away.'

'And what did you do when the soldiers took your car away?'

'What could I have done? I just kept walking.'

'See what I mean. That's what's wrong. Nobody fights back. Our property is taken and our children are violated and what do we do? We take one look at the guns and bullets and we run like mad. We don't want to die. Well, I'll tell you something else. We're dead already. At least you and your likes. Oh I saw them at the barrier. "Yes, sir, no, sir. Thank you very much, sir." They must get to their work, protect their families. What you don't know is that when those soldier fellows start shooting they follow no logical pattern. As one cynic once put it, when it comes to shooting, bullets are not directed against anybody, they are fired "to whom it may concern". In theory your family should be in as much danger as my own then. Regardless of what we individually might have done.' Moses stopped and his eyes searched for the bottle of brandy.

'The same danger! Is it really?' Joe was not going to tell the details. Something made him want to suppress these facts, get them the hell out of his life. No, he was not saying anything, not to a stranger. The story would spread after some time all right; but it would not have come from him. So he just sat and looked at Moses, his thoughts flashing off in all sorts of directions! Jesus, that man in the house! Really! Now there is a man for you. Only those who didn't see him would think that God had no sense of humour. Was that what Chesterton said about hippopotamuses? Christ Almighty! But had he not himself accused the crowds at the barrier of exactly the same thing which Moses was accusing him of now? So how could he prove that he did not submit to these cruelties except by actually fighting? Must a man be dragged to that level to prove a point?

'More brandy?' Moses said, bottle poised to pour.

'Thanks, I really do need some.'

The brandy poured into the glass. Its bouquet hit Joe's nose as he brought the glass to the mouth, but it missed his reflexes. This was not brandy to savour, this was brandy to hold on to.

'Yes, Joe, if we don't fight in time, you'll find your relations killed and your mother raped; and then it'll be almost too late to fight. For then you'll never know when you fight whether you are fighting for principle or for personal grudge.'

This was really too much for Joe. It was all falling into place. How could this man know all these details? He must have killed his relatives and raped Joe's mother. Yes it must be him or else how could he know? Soldiers? His mother must have been taken in by hooligans in the same way as Joe himself had been taken in. Anger swelled in Joe's breast. His head reeled and his blood burnt. His eyes were hot embers as he rose from the chair; the pain in his knee had completely vanished.

Moses sensed trouble and began to move backwards. Joe was a bigger man and well fed. Tension filled the room. The placid Akolo hugged the wall, afraid to fall. The fierce figures in the Sserulyo seemed to raise their spears ready for the attack. On the floor the red carpet flowed and waited to receive blood. Ghosts in the wind moved behind the curtains, shaking them slightly. Small Nigerian sculptures, with nails in their eyes seemed to hold their breath.

'I'll kill you, Moses, I'll kill you,' Joe screamed, and charged after Moses like a wounded lion. 'You massacred my relations and raped my mother. I'll kill you and the whole of your stinking lot.' Moses had no time to protest his innocence; he ran across the room attempting to get the sofa between him and Joe. But Joe jumped over it and landed on his bottom on the side. Moses moved from behind the sofa and ran to the window shouting for help.

He did not make it to the wall; he tripped over a rug and fell. Joe hurled himself after him and fell on top of his body. He grabbed his throat and tried to squeeze the air out of it, but Moses managed to push the menacing arms aside.

'Don't kill me, Joe. You're mad. I didn't kill your relations. I don't even know where your home is.'

'Don't lie to me. Where are the rest of your thieving bastards. You were at my house first, and one of you knocked me on the head with a gun. Now come on talk before I kill you.'

'You're mad, Joe, you're mad. And if you kill me they'll hang you.'

'I'm not mad. And if I'm mad then they'll not hang me after I have killed you. Now, what were you doing in the country in that disguise? Is that the way you get your money? By raping old women and stealing their property? And then you lie about the bricks and the house . . .'

'Look, I tell you, honest. I stole the bricks from the government supplies and I didn't kill any of your relations. I only went to the country . . . Now let me up and I'll explain.'

But Joe pressed against Moses and grabbed his throat again. He squeezed it till the life nearly shot out. Suddenly he came to his senses. He released his grasp and Moses held his neck where Joe's hands had been. He was breathing with difficulty but realized he had to explain quickly or not at all.

'Listen, honest. It was dark when we passed the trench, remember. I was the only one who got out of the car. So you didn't see what I saw. There were bodies of soldiers all around. Well I dug the trench. That's all I did. That's all I do. Dig trenches. I gave up persuading intellectuals like yourself to join the fight against this . . . this rot in the nation, and decided to do whatever I could whenever I could. So what I do, whenever there is a *coup d'état*, I go and dig a trench for the soldiers to fall in. That's all I do: dig a trench in the middle of the road.'

Joe stopped and looked at his hands as if it was the first time he had noticed the fingered contraptions at the ends of his arms. He could not believe his own violence. He lifted his weight off Moses and stood up. Then he began to move back, stepping away carefully with his back to the wall. Confusion filled his mind. He was caught between several emotions none of which could actually gain control of him and establish a clear pattern of reaction and behaviour. There was so much he could not understand because he never let himself look at it properly as he always suppressed it. And there was Moses, a man he had been trying to kill. Moses had just done what he, Joe, wanted to do so many times but kept putting off and rationalizing out of existence. But how did Moses know about the raping? That he still had to find out. Was it because Joe wanted to revenge the fate of his family that he had attempted to kill Moses believing he was guilty of this crime? Or was it because Moses had mentioned something for which Joe basically blamed himself. 'If more of us had done our duty before, there would not be so much room for so many stupid imbeciles to become politicians.' Joe had preferred his comfort? And now Moses was saying that if he, Joe, would not do his duty, then . . . Oh, hell, it has all happened already. So why bother at all now? But who can live in a country like that and with a conscience such as he had now? All these years; and such wasted time and talent; the missed opportunities. The private sins and all the superb inabilities imposed by a many-sided talent. But he could not use them all. However, he should have come to terms with the fact, but he always externalized. Of course it was not him, it was just the imbecilities of the society in which he lived. Why write books, or paint pictures or design beautiful houses? Some idiot is bound to come and burn the lot. So save yourself the bother. Design the end result, not the middle stage, just the ruins; write on the ashes, build graves with bodies in them, write silent symphonies and ... Oh hell! That's why he could never understand why God had to create bodies, send them to earth, kill them and extract their souls to take them back to heaven. Why could he not create souls and keep them in heaven in the first place? Or is he a farmer of souls: plants them into earthly bodies and waits for the harvest? Or are souls wines, and the bodies the casks in which they have to mature? Then why not brew a mature wine in the first place? So it is all for nothing. You cannot have perfection, for there is no logic to things, only chaos. You are only sure of two things: death and the present moment. You make the best of one, while you have it, and wait for the other. He had been before through all this reasoning, if that is what you could call it. So why again? And why now?

'Moses.'

'Yes, Joe,' Moses spoke haltingly.

'How did you know about the raping?'

'What raping?'

'You've just said. How did you know my mother was . . . ?' He could not bring himself to say it.

'Joe, was she . . . ?'

Joe shook his head in slow vertical motions.

'Oh God, I'm sorry. But I didn't know it. I was only making a point of argument. Oh hell! I heard the soldiers had been that way but I heard no crying as I picked you up. That's where your home is, isn't it?'

'Well a little distance from there. But there was no crying. Just silence. They came to my house too. Five men. I could've been killed, but the radio surprised them. They knocked me on the head, and I didn't go to the country till the shadows had spoken to me.'

'The shadows?'

'Yes, perhaps if the shadows had not detained me with their confessions, I could've got to my mother's home before the soldiers. And then they might have killed me as well. I don't know now which would have been better.'

'Did you say the shadows?' Moses was a little worried about Joe's health.

'Yes, I did. It's a place not far from where man stands, yet few ever get there to testify. Inner cleanliness, that's what humanity needs. Not a lot of deodorized exteriors. Will you take me home now?'

'Are you sure you are feeling all right?'

'No. I'm depressed and perplexed, but otherwise I'm O.K.'

'My friend Stephen. We might call by his house. He's head of the psychiatric department at the Government Hospital. He might have some drugs at the house with him.' That was a little tactless, but well meant.

'He can go shrink his own head. Anyway I don't trust these new-fangled fellows any more. Psychiatrists are born, not made. I believe in only two types: the biochemist and the good old traditional doctor. Do you still call him witch doctor?'

'Don't ...'

'That's old-fashioned. It went out with the Europeans, the khaki shorts and the helmet.'

'But I think you ought ...'

'You don't believe me? Look here, I'll give you his telephone number.' He paused. 'He's on the telephone. No use getting a witch doctor unless you can reach him by telephone. Nice young man this one. Better than anyone I've met. He can get to your subconscious in a flash and get out those phobias for you, your enemies he calls them. Once you can face them, everything is O.K. And he does not verbalize about it. Not like your American types. He is intuitive. Inherited it from his grandfather but, by jove, at a pound a session you get your money's worth. I met him through Simon my servant. He was a friend of the witchdoctor's chauffeur. Nice young man.' The mention of Simon checked his mounting enthusiasm. He looked morose again: 'Do you think they'll kill him?'

'No, I don't think so. Er ... I mean they don't kill witch doctors any more,' Moses answered, not noticing the change of subject.

'No, not him. I mean Simon.'

'Oh sorry. No, I hope not.'

They fell silent for a while. One of those moments when two minds dig around a subject and meet at the other end. They did not say anything about it, but they felt they knew what to do.

'Give me your phone number.'

'Take my phone number.'

The two men spoke together. After he had noted the number Joe got up to leave. He held his knee as that pain returned with a vengeance. 'Ever had a bad knee, Moses?'

'No, Joe.'

'Too bad; then you can't suggest a cure?'

They went out of the house and drove off in the Mercedes in the direction of Joe's house. He reflected that the arrest of Simon would be a great setback to the search. But if he could find that 'soldier's' uniform, he would probably be able to trace Yacobo. Then he would ask the engineer Moses to help him 'arrest' Stephen and Matthew. They he could bring face to face with Yacobo and press him to testify against them.

9 Yacobo and Jeronimo got up early to go and look for the uniform. Jeronimo had to be found something to wear.

'Try this one on.'

'No, I don't want it. It'll look ridiculous on me.'

'It'll look ridiculous all right with those squatting shoulders of yours, but it'll get you past the police. Now try it.'

'I said I don't want it. Why don't you go and get the clothes by yourself.'

'How do you like that? Me, Yacobo, go and get Jeronimo's clothes by myself because he was stupid enough to leave his poll tax tickets in them.'

'Well, it was your idea to go and . . .'

'Shut up. Was it also my idea to go to the toilet and wake up the servant?'

'I had to go to the toilet or I should have . . .'

'All right, now, what do you prefer: wet trousers or jail? You're going to wear what I'm giving you, and you and I are going back to that house and get those clothes.'

Jeronimo looked away for a moment and then snatched the garment from Yacobo's hand. He wore it. Yacobo looked at him and chuckled. They walked out of the house.

'Don't forget to bring me some salt when you return,' Rozalia shouted from the kitchen.

'Honestly, that woman and her salt . . .' He paused. 'I hope those clothes are still there, for your sake.'

'And yours.'

'Shut up.' He paused again. 'Jeronimo, maybe you have a better memory than I have, could you remind me to buy some salt on our way back?'

'Yes.'

'Thanks.'

The sun meant nothing in Yacobo's slum area, except in as far as it helped to dry the rot. Its rising beauty highlighted the ugliness of the falling shacks. Its light revealed the dirt. Its warmth reminded one of the coldness within

152

oneself. As Jeronimo and Yacobo walked away in the early morning, they took one look at the sun and knew it was there; they could ignore it till it went to sleep again.

They wound along the slummy byways. The smell of rubbish and urine filled the air. Pot-bellied children squatted on the mud verandas of the shacks. Lean dogs scrounged around for the faeces. It made a man's stomach turn. Some acquiesced in it and ascribed it to fate. Others tried hard to adapt to it by entertaining hope of salvation from it; and a few revolted against it. But those that revolted lacked a co-ordinated direction of effort and feeling. No common explanation or plan of attack emerged so that each individual was left to create his own scape-goat. Of these there were many; such as the rich, the missionaries, the colonialists, the foreigners. The solutions were equally isolated and divergent. For Yacobo and Jeronimo it was a revolt against society and the good things in it. They felt denied and deprived so they took what they found. They did not love what they did but it was an outlet for frustrated talent, desire and ambition. So far they had been lucky and had not been overtaken by the sanctions of society. Maybe if someone came with a co-ordinated solution, made them feel useful, showed them an opportunity, and revealed to them that their position was not entirely without hope, then they could be saved from themselves and the terrible rancour that slowly gnawed at their insides. Somebody like that had still to show up. There were not many good people left around. In the meantime they were fair game for recruitment as political thugs. They reached the precipice which separated their neighbourhood from the one in which Joe lived. They climbed it helping each other. Joe's house was not far.

'If you see any suspicious eyes, ignore them. If they ask questions we are gardeners. Right?'

'Right,' Jeronimo replied, uneasily.

In the valley below them they could see what appeared to be army trucks, with a number of people busily around them. But in this fashionable neighbourhood where they were now, everything was quiet and the flowers bloomed and the bees picked up pollen.

'Now which rose bush were you squatting under?'

'Can't remember, it was dark.'

'Look out; some people are coming.'

Yacobo and Jeronimo pretended to be gardeners: 'The best fertilizers on the market are too expensive for some types of flowers. I'll tell you what I use . . .'

'How do you mean they are too expensive, I mean anything for a flower. I can't say how roses like these couldn't be worth any fertilizer in the world.'

'That new insecticide, now I don't think . . .'

The people passed and the two men were themselves again:

'Now try to use that head of yours. Where did you leave the clothes?'

'Wait a minute. The banana leaves. Where is the banana tree?'

They moved over to an almost bare banana tree; and there down by the stalk were Jeronimo's clothes. They picked them up and hurried away.

'You probably killed that man,' Jeronimo said.

'What?'

154

'I said you probably killed that man. His car wasn't in the garage. The curtains were pulled and even his servant wasn't anywhere around.'

'Now, shut up and stop scaring me. Anyway, how will they find out? If he said anything, he only saw soldiers not us.'

'He isn't that daft, you know. He must've seen the way we behaved when the announcement came. You panicked.'

'All right, all right and stop being so bloody morose about it. If he's dead then he can't talk, can he?'

They jumped down the precipice again and headed for the slum.

'The salt.'

'The what?'

'I said the salt.'

'That's right, the salt.'

They entered a small shop.

'Well, you've got the money.' Yacobo said to Jeronimo.

'What money? I haven't any money. I left it in the . . .'

'We've just got your clothes back. Now get the money and buy some salt.'

Jeronimo dipped his hand in the pocket of the trousers he carried. He got out twenty-five cents and bought a pound of salt.

'Anything else?'

They left the shop to walk home. As they approached their neighbourhood, they noticed an excited atmosphere. People spoke in loud voices and gesticulated vigorously. Then they heard people crying and wailing. 'What's going on?' they demanded of a man who passed them. He looked at the uniform Jeronimo was carrying in his hand. He made as if to run.

'Come on, don't be afraid. I said what the hell is going on here?'

'The soldiers. It's the soldiers. They've been here. They said they were looking for thugs. And when we told them we didn't know of any thugs, they took ten people out in the market and shot them right under our very noses.'

'Who, who did they shoot?' Yacobo and Jeronimo were trembling.

'Oh, please don't ask me. I don't know their names. They just took any ten people from the shops and shot them,' he sobbed.

Yacobo and Jeronimo left him and ran off at great speed to Yacobo's house.

'Rozalia! Rozalia!' There was no answer. 'It can't be. They can't do it. God help them if they've done it. They can't . . .'

'Let's go to the market-place. Maybe she went there when she heard the shooting.' Jeronimo pulled Yacobo, who was getting panic-stricken. They ran off to the market at great speed, with Yacobo still yelling out: 'Rozalia! Rozalia! Can you hear me . . . ?'

In the market-place there was a heap of bodies. Yacobo pushed past everybody and anybody who happened to be in his way. He reached the heap of human flesh. One by one and at great speed he pulled away the dead and the dying. He screamed in agony. She lay there in a pool of blood, barely alive. In her hand she held a parcel. He called out to her 'Rozalia, Rozalia . . .' She could not answer. She raised her feeble eyes and indicated the parcel in her hand. Yacobo grabbed it and burst it open. It was a pound of salt. They looked at each other and she attempted a smile. Then she fell back and was silent. Yacobo bent his head and stopped breathing. Something stopped him from within. It was pushing up his throat. Then he wailed: 'Woowe, woowe, Rozalia don't go. Don't leave me.'

People turned round and looked at him. A young woman came and squatted beside him and joined in the crying. He did not see her; he did not know her, just a woman moved to tears.

Jeronimo stood voiceless. He remembered the army uniform he had in his hand. He was petrified. He must get away immediately; if anybody mistook him for the army at a moment like this, he was a dead man. But what about Yacobo? He could not leave him behind. He would never be able to find his way home in his present state. He stopped for a moment. Then he decided that all he had to do was to pull Yacobo away and run him home and burn the uniform. No sooner had he made a move than one rough-hewn young man stopped him

'What's that in your hand?'

'Er, er . . . ?'

'That's a uniform. You're one of them, aren't you?'

'No, I'm not. I just have this to . . .'

'Here's one of them. They left him behind to spy.' The people gathered round Jeronimo.

'Who are you? You swine. Lynch him . . .'

'I tell you honestly I'm not a soldier.'

'Who does he think he's lying to? That face and that uniform.'

'He's one of them. Kill him.'

'Honestly, ask Yacobo. Yacobo, tell them about this uniform.'

'Rozalia, Rozalia, oh, they've killed my wife. They've killed her . . . oh . . .'

'Yacobo, tell them. They will kill me. Tell them what we were doing with this uniform.'

'Oh, Rozalia . . .'

'Kill him, kill him, he's a soldier. He killed our people.' The crowd pounced on Jeronimo with sticks and stones and bottles and anything they could get their hands on. He fell under the weight of violence. He was bleeding all over. 'Tell them, Yacobo, tell them what we . . .' And the life went out of him. They took his body and tied a rope around his neck. Then they hung it up from a tree in the market-place. The vultures gathered, and the people began to go home.

Yacobo did not know what had happened to Jeronimo. He got up automatically when he saw everybody leave. Slowly he walked back to his house, his pound of salt still in his hand. He kept muttering to himself, 'Rozalia, Rozalia, I've brought the salt.'

10 It took fifteen minutes for Joe and Moses to arrive at Joe's house. Mvule Hill was the apex of society in Adnagu in at least one respect: success. It did not particularly matter what the man had succeeded at.

Top civil servants, corrupt politicians, businessmen and the Archbishop all lived there. It was here, at the eternal cocktail parties, that businessmen and politicians exchanged directorships for guarantees of Government contracts and 'informed' advice. Young ladies went to Mvule Hill every evening to explore the frontiers between love and prostitution. There were gold and diamonds in the hills between these frontiers, and a discreet prospector could open up her mine and keep a good name at the same time. The public saw only what the press photographers allowed them to see: fat men with whisky glasses in their hands busy 'directing the business of the nation'. At Mvule Hill, good and evil were reconciled in success.

Joe had no time to waste. He had planned to rest briefly and to change his shirt but, as soon as he saw his house, he changed his mind. This thing had to be done straight away.

'Moses, you can forget my telephone number; we'll start work right away.'

'How do you mean?'

'I mean come in and I'll explain the plan.'

Moses had intended to drop Joe, go to town, do some shopping, and return to his house before curfew hours. He did not protest as he was led into the house. It was as Joe had left it; Simon had cleaned it well. They opened the windows and the scent of roses came in from the back garden. Flowers always smelled good even in a cemetery. Joe dispensed with courtesies and got straight down to business. He explained to Moses the whole story about Stephen, Matthew, the butcher and Yacobo. The trust between the two men grew with every minute.

As it would soon be dark, they decided that Moses should drive to town and get a curfew pass: that would enable them to finish their business in the night. Moses left and Joe started looking in the back garden for the uniform. He looked everywhere; in the flower bushes, under the hedges, in the dustbin. He could find nothing. He was about to give up the search when two of his neighbours saw him.

'He has come back very quickly this time,' one of them said to the other. 'Must be getting more courageous. Normally he is away for two weeks after a *coup d'état*. Let's go and talk to him.' They went up to Joe where he stood wondering whether there was any place in which to look.

'Welcome back, Joe. I say, you have come back quickly this time.'

'That's the trouble with this place,' Joe said in irritation. 'Nobody minds their own business, unless it hurts nobody if they do.'

'All right, all right, Joe, don't bite your lips off your mouth. As you like. We were only trying to be neighbourly.'

'Well, you can go and neighbourize with yourselves. I'm not interested.'

'I said, as you please. We didn't come to beg food from you. If a man can't live with his neighbours, then what's the point of worrying about the society and the nation, and all those things you *used* to tell us about.'

'If you don't leave me alone, I'll have to say something very rude to you.'

'Why don't you leave him alone? You can never tell with people these days. Must we lose sleep over another man's stomach ache,' the man who had been silent said to his friend.

'All right, I'm trying one more time before I give up.'

'Must you?'

'Yes,' and then turning to Joe. 'I say you've some lovely flowers, Joe. Can you let me have one of those gardeners of yours for my roses?'

'Why my garden? Let's talk about dogs; they're as good a way to start off a stunted conversation. Since when have I had gardeners?'

'Is that the new trend? Denying your luxuries? Mind you I don't blame you. What with all the socialist nonsense thrown about these days, you might be taken as one of the *bourgeoisie* when the revolution comes. Still you needn't worry about me.'

'Has the new moon arrived? What kind of madness is getting into your head?'

'Madness? I was going to say the same thing to you, only I was more careful. Who is mad then? You or me?' Then he turned to his friend, 'Didn't we see two gardeners here yesterday or am I going mad?'

'You're not going mad because we did see two gardeners here. But I should say you're going mad because you love to take rudeness from people. Let's go,' the other replied.

Joe was struck by a sudden insight. 'Hold on a minute. Did you say you saw two gardeners here?'

'Isn't that what I said?' one of the men said to the other.

'Yes we did see them here,' they addressed themselves to Joe. 'There were two men in your garden, talking about fertilizers and roses. Sounded very intelligent for the normal kind of gardener, that's why I was saying . . .'

'What did they look like?'

'Oh . . . like gardeners, you know. They were looking under the rose bushes so we saw more of their rears than their fronts. But going by their buttocks I would say they were two tall men.'

'Did you see where they went when they had finished?'

'Well, not exactly; but we think they went down the Kisenyi slums, don't we?' one said addressing the last question to his friend.

Joe had not felt such excitement for years. He was almost trembling. He moved up to the two men, he was biting his teeth, making the muscles on his jaws expand. His face was intense. He took the hands of the men without asking and shook them. 'Thank you very much. I'll never forget this. Thank you,' he said and walked away almost in tears.

'Poor man,' said one of the men. 'Too much pressure on the brain. He ought to see a doctor before it gets worse.'

Joe returned to his sitting-room and waited for Moses. He arrived back after a short while with a curfew pass in his hand. Joe explained immediately that they would have to drive to the Kisenyi and see if they could find the two men.

'But I mean, how do we start?' Moses asked.

'I know the name of one of them. At least I think it's him. So we'll start from there.'

They got into the Mercedes. Its tyres crushed the husks of the seeds of the jacaranda trees scattered in the boulevard. They would never bear the flower, for they had fallen and wasted their lives on the hot tarmac. It was getting dark now and they kept the curfew pass handy. Probably they would never have been able to find Yacobo, whom they knew as Katende, if it had not been for the army killings of Rozalia and the civilians in the Kisenyi and the subsequent mob-murder of Jeronimo. They heard the story at the first beer hall at which they stopped.

'I'd say that it was a great pity, because he wasn't a soldier at all,' said a man after he had drunk a glass of banana beer and spat the millet seeds into the corner of the house. 'But he had it coming to him. Him and that ruffian Yacobo had to come to some harm one day. If you swallow thorns today, you must expect your anus to hurt tomorrow. No, it's the poor woman. She was a decent girl before she married him. It's only her I really am sorry about.'

So one of them was dead. Still there were four more, Joe thought. He did not know that the other three were shot in the night as they fled, and that, in fact, only Yacobo remained. Still if he found him, there was hope.

'Where does this other man Yacobo live?' Joe asked.

'What do you want him for?' the drunk asked.

'He's a friend of ours.'

'Then you must know where he lives.' He drunk again, spat and wiped his mouth with his hand. 'I tell you if a man mixed the red earth of an anthill in water and urinated in it, you'd never be able to tell the difference between that and this beer. I've been robbed.' Two men across the room agreed with him, but ordered some more.

'Would you like another glass yourself?' Joe asked the man.

'Do I move away my farm when it starts to rain? Mind

you it is hardly worth the effort it takes to swallow the stuff. But I'll not insult your kindness.'

Joe ordered a glass for him. Moses knew what Joe was up to and, if it had not been for the circumstances, he would have reminded him of their conversation about the Nigerian customs officer. The glass was placed before the man and Joe looked at him. 'Where does that man Yacobo live?'

'I told you; I'm not a singing bird. I don't live on millet seeds.' He spat another mouthful of seeds and reached out for the glass. Joe moved away the drink before the man got to it. They looked at each other for a tense moment, then he gave in: 'All right, all right, every man for himself. The fifth house in this row. And don't say I told you so.' They let him have his drink. As they walked out, he looked at them and said: 'And mind how you go, the men in these areas have no respect for the paths along which they walk.'

They reached the house. But now they had to bring Stephen and Matthew. If they left the house unattended, people, probably the drunk himself, might warn Yacobo. They thought for a while.

'All right, Moses. Let's do it this way. You stay here and guard the house, I'll take your car and get Stephen and Matthew.'

'You're feeling very strong today, or else you have the death wish on you.'

'Don't worry. I'll manage. I know their ways.' Moses pleaded with Joe but he would not listen, so he let him go.

Joe drove back to his house and got the pistol. Stephen and Matthew lived in the Kimuli quarters where the middle rank civil servants mostly had their houses. It took Joe only a few minutes to get to Stephen's house. He knocked at the door. They must have been plotting something or else congratulating themselves, Joe thought. For, after the servant had opened the door, Joe entered to find both men seated in the sitting-room. There were signs of fear on their faces as they looked at Joe. He stood and stared at them, and as he did, he felt the strength and cunning of his earlier life return to him. The first thing to do was to get rid of the servant.

'Hallo, friends,' Joe said, pretending as well as he could to sound jovial. 'You were expecting me, were you? Well I've thought about it. Pride doesn't pay. And principles, they have limits too. It's many years since we disagreed, but I've come to realize that our quarrel hurts nobody but us and benefits nobody but our enemies. So I've come to talk over everything.' He looked round for a chair and sat on its arm.

Matthew was silent. Then Stephen stirred as if he had just noticed the silence. 'Boy, what are you standing there for. Go and get my friend Joe a drink.'

The boy turned and went to the kitchen. As soon as he was in the kitchen, Joe swiftly backed up to the kitchen door and locked it behind him. At the same time he produced a pistol.

'I said I've come to talk. But we aren't going to talk here. We shall need some other people to help us along.' He stopped and looked at them. He could not really tell what the two men were thinking. They seemed to be staring at him, undecided as to what their reaction should be. Did they think he knew what they had done? Or had they in fact done nothing and were thinking that Joe wanted to kill them so that he might take all the guns. Maybe it was one of his practical jokes. He just wanted to measure them up. Anyway what the hell was going on?

Then Joe moved. He took a rope which he had brought with him from his house, and threw it to Stephen: 'Now pick it up, slowly.'

Stephen had no alternative but to follow the order mechanically until he understood exactly what was going on.

'Tie Matthew's hands behind his back. Then the two of you will walk slowly in front of me to the car outside.' Stephen looked Matthew in the face as if saying: 'Come on, it is not my fault, but I have to do it.' Matthew put his hands behind him, almost without thought. When they were ready, Joe told them with a movement of his gun to walk ahead of him. He told Stephen to sit in the driver's seat and sat in the back seat with Matthew.

'Now drive strictly on my instructions. If you meet a police barrier, stop. The curfew pass is in the glove compartment. Now start the car.'

Stephen drove carefully. Maybe he still did not believe Joe was serious, or maybe he did and was looking for an opportunity to leap. But Joe held the gun ready and no man can act independently in front of death. Soon they were in the Kisenyi. The car lights caught the dark figure of Moses who, in his worry for Joe's life had been bending and touching his knees for support, squatting briefly, and then walking around in a small circle back to where he had squatted.

He raised his head from a bending position and looked

at the car as it stopped. Recognizing it as his Mercedes, he walked carefully up to it and was relieved to see Joe in the back seat. He did know Stephen well, so at first he thought Joe had got a driver to help him. He opened the door and Joe came out, his gun carefully trained at Stephen who had his hands free. He backed up slowly and asked them to come out of the car. Moses looked on. 'Get a rope and tie the other one as well.' After looking round and finding no rope, Moses settled for holding Stephen's hands behind his back. They approached the door of the house.

'Open up there!' Joe shouted, but there was no reply, though he could see a small light through a crack in the wall. 'Open up, do you hear me.' Silence.

'Will somebody tell me what is going on?' said Stephen.

'If you shut your mouth you will find out,' replied Joe without looking at him. He paused for a second. Then moved back and kicked the door in with his right leg. A small paraffin light stood in the centre of what looked like a bare room. Its flame bent over to one side as the wind rushed into the room.

Moses and Joe pushed their men in first and then followed them. It was a small room which smelled of rotting flesh. In the corner a human figure crouched with its back to them and was digging away furiously at the mud at the base of the wall. Particles of earth flew back as the elbows moved back and forwards like pistons. Nobody knew exactly how to take this as they all stood and looked. Then the man in the corner looked up over his shoulder at them. He shuddered slightly and attempted to cover his face with his arms. Was this Yacobo or not? His face could barely be seen in the light of the small paraffin lamp.

Joe moved slowly in a semi-circle, picked up the light and held it in the man's face. It was him all right, the man he had seen at his house, and the very Katende who years ago forced him to say the name of that weed.

After a pause as the two men looked at one another, Yacobo said: 'Now you see what you have done! You've made him run away.' Nobody knew what he was talking about. 'Well don't just stand there, follow him in the hole. I was digging him up when you came and made that noise with the door. Now I'll never find him.'

'Who?' Joe attempted to understand.

'How should I know? I was sitting here all by myself when he came in, walked across the room and entered the hole there. Now that's no good, is it?'

'No, it's . . . hell what am I talking about. Now stop fooling around. We aren't deceived you know,' Joe said. 'Tell us what you did to the butcher and who sent you to do it.'

'Honestly it's not my fault. I brought the salt. My wife should have waited here. Look, here's the salt. I told her I would bring it one day.' He paused and then said, 'Would you care for a grain of salt?'

'The man's sick, let's leave him,' Moses said to Joe.

'Are you crazy, Moses? Then what'll we do with these two? Anyway he's all right, he's only trying to deceive us. Now you there tell me: Who killed the butcher?'

Stephen and Matthew were silent and showed no emotion. The man looked up, shook his head in confusion and said:

'How should I know? Go ask the butcher.'

'But the butcher's dead, you fool.'

'Which fool? You never said he was dead, all you said was that they had killed him.'

'Moses, what are we talking about?' Joe turned to his friend rubbing his face with the back of his hand.

'I told you the man's sick.' They thought for a short while.

'There are two rats in that hole,' the man said. This stirred Joe as he tried to figure out what was happening and he looked strangely puzzled. 'I said there are two rats in that hole. And he went in there too. That ought to teach him a lesson.' He attempted to laugh. Joe looked at him with a confusion of feelings: resignation, disgust and confused despair. So there he was, big Katende with his knuckles, digging two big rats and an unknown man out of a hole in his house. Maybe next minute he would enter the hole himself, to complete the journey, and even find a final rest.

'Joe, let's get out of here,' Moses said sensing the despair in the air. But Joe was still staring at Yacobo Katende, Stephen, and Matthew. What good was it? As if by some involuntary act of his whole system, Joe's fingers opened and the gun fell out of his hand. Moses began to walk out and Joe followed him mechanically. The others stayed in the house.

Outside, the rot and decay of the neighbourhood pervaded the air. 'Where are we going next, Joe?' Moses asked. Joe just looked at him and shrugged his shoulders. There was a brief silence and then Moses said: 'Do you think it was them? Do you think those three were responsible for the death of the butcher?'

'Does it matter?' Joe said, almost absent-mindedly.

169

'Like hell it doesn't! Jesus, why do we bother then? What were we looking for anyway?' Moses was feeling the anger rise in his chest.

'Do you want to know who killed the butcher and his family?' Joe asked, suddenly becoming alive again. 'And do you want to know who raped my mother and killed the children? Who drove Katende mad and then started looking for him to kill him? Do you want to know? Well I'll tell you. We did. You and I, and this whole goddam society. It's greed, barriers, unformed pseudo-philosophies and God knows what.'

'Ah come on,' said Moses. 'That kind of sweeping conclusion is probably as useless and perhaps even more dangerous than the rest of scheming humanity. In the end it can even be downright irresponsible. It's the beginning of a total resignation; a complete loss of hope. And if we cannot hope any more we might as well start digging our own graves.'

'You're damn right about the graves. In the end perhaps death will be our only saving grace.' Joe stopped for a moment and then added: 'I don't know what you're going to do next, Moses, but I'm going back to my mother's place for the funeral. I must bury the dead.'

'Yes,' Moses agreed automatically.

'Moses?'

'Yes, Joe.'

'Do you understand what's going on? I mean can you stand there and tell me you can still tell sanity from madness; or even dare to recognize sanity in the actions of humanity without losing it in yourself?'

'I don't know, Joe. Let me come with you to the funeral.

We must dig more trenches, and there is a nice place where I'll dig one straight after the funeral. You know how it is. I mean I've got to do something, haven't I?' He asked more of himself than Joe.

They started to go, and as they went, Joe's hand went to his thigh to take a note but he found that he had nothing to say.